IN THE STARS

By J. Karter

Independently published by J. Karter
Printed in the USA

This is a work of fiction. Names, characters, places, and events are products of the author's imagination or are used fictitiously. Any resemblance to actual events, locales, or persons, living or dead, is entirely coincidental.

Scripture quotation taken from the Holy Bible, New International Version®, NIV®, © 1973, 1978, 1984, 2011 by Biblica, Inc.™ Used by permission. All rights reserved worldwide.

© 2025
All rights reserved
ISBN-13: 979-8-9931322-0-4
Edited by Elizabeth Trotter

In the Stars by J. Karter

People look at the outward appearance,
but the Lord looks at the heart.
1 Samuel 16:7

In the Stars • J. Karter

Chapter 1
Ian

"Is your dad seriously going to make you do this?"

I glare over at Ethan. He should know that answer. "How many years have you known me again?"

"Eight years this fall," he says proudly.

"And has my dad ever gone back on something he wants?"

"No, not that I can remember."

"And why do you think that would start now?" My voice is laced with sarcasm and annoyance at his optimism.

"A guy can dream, right?"

"Not when this is reality," I sigh as I feel my car shift into park.

"Well, do you want to help me go through auditions?"

"For what?"

"That new movie the studio is working on. A bunch of people sent in auditions, and I need to make sure they fit what the director is looking for."

"What exactly is he looking for?" I ask, getting out and following Ethan to his apartment.

"Blonde and short," he says, fiddling with his keys.

"Seriously?"

"There are other things he wants, but my job is to find someone blonde and short," he says as we walk inside, disappearing into the other room.

"Well, that can't be too hard." I sit down on the couch.

"Great, here's your box," he says, setting a milk crate down in front of me. I stare at them. Each one seems to have more files than the last.

"I think your boss gave you the never-ending job," I say with a laugh. He just shakes his head. It takes two hours, but I think we get them into two piles: ones that fit the description and ones that don't.

"Did you find any that interested you?" Ethan smirks.

I look at him, confused. "What?"

"I mean, if you have to find a girlfriend, you might as well date an actress," he says with a shrug.

"Yeah, because that's what I need in my life: an actress who's full of herself and just using me to boost her social status."

"I mean, when you think about it, you are kinda using her too. All you need her for is the publicity of this song."

"What if I don't just want a girl for the publicity of this song, though? What if I want something real? Someone I could see a future with?"

Ethan lets out a sad sigh and looks over at me. He gives me a look that I've become all too familiar with. Something that borders on pity but reminds me that this is the life I have chosen for myself.

"Ian, you don't have the luxury of that right now. Your dad wants the fake girlfriend, so pay an actress, let her collect the check, and go your separate ways."

I feel myself getting frustrated and heartbroken knowing he's right. It just needs to be a temporary arrangement.

"Find a girl; it only needs to last a month, right? It takes you an average of a month to write and produce a song. You'll have it recorded, announce the relationship, and break up because of the pressure of the media. It's a single, not an album; it's a quick turnaround."

"Fine, I'll find one. It's only one month, right?" I mumble under my breath.

"Yeah, I think that should satisfy your dad. It just needs to be until the publicity dies down."

"Yeah, because publicity always follows a nice, neat schedule," I mutter. He glares at me. I roll my eyes and help Ethan load the boxes back into his car.

"Do you want to run these back to the office with me?"

"Sure, why not? I have nothing better to do on this Friday night."

"We are so lame," Ethan says with a laugh as we climb into his car. I begin to get lost in my thoughts as we drive down the quiet roads. Is finding someone real ever going to be something that is an option for me? Then again, do I even remember what real is at this point?

We drive into town and pull into the parking garage underneath the building. It's closed, so unless you have a key card, you can't get in. We go inside and take the elevator up to Ethan's office.

We walk inside and stack all the boxes over in the corner. As I am stacking boxes, a folder on the table catches my eye. "Who is this?" I ask.

Ethan looks up from what he's doing to see the photo. "I don't know, some girl who didn't get her stuff in on time. Her audition must have come in after I left," he says as if he's brushing her off.

There's a short pause as we both look at her picture. Her hair's a little messy, and she's looking away from the camera.

I look at the other two pictures she submitted. In one, she's staring intently into the camera, and in the other, she looks as if she's almost mid-laugh. There's something about her eyes, or maybe it's her smile, that makes her stand out against the rest of them.

"She doesn't fit the description either, so just put it with the rejects," Ethan says as he walks back across the room.

"Can I get her information?" I blurt out.

"Why, does she look less like an actress to you?" he asks with a laugh.

I can't help but smile looking at her pictures. "No, but she does look . . . real."

Ethan gets up and walks back over to me. "You know I can't give you any information on her. I wish I could, but you know I can't."

I nod my head, understanding. He takes a deep breath. "I really can't tell you that her manager's information is on the back of her headshot." I turn over the photo and take a picture of the back. "Or the fact that her manager is really good at returning calls within business hours."

I take a mental note of everything he is saying. Once I get home for the night, I copy all of the information down onto a sticky note and leave it in my dad's office.

"Step one, complete," I whisper to myself with a grin as I quietly close the door. It will be a few weeks before we get everything figured out, but at least now I know the girl.

Chapter 2
Avalon

No one ever told me making it in Hollywood would be easy. I mean, to be fair, they all told me the exact opposite. I just didn't think it would be this hard.

I sit there on my bed, looking at the TV in my small studio apartment. I turn on the TV, quickly glancing at each passing channel, praying that my street doesn't end up on a breaking news update. I should have noticed the place was cheap; I was just glad I could actually afford rent somewhere. Well, I used to be able to.

I glance over at the table that is now covered with bills. I let out a sigh and try to distract myself from the fact that I'm going home in three weeks. That's when this lease is up. I never really liked growing up in Kansas, but at least I was in a better situation than I'm in right now.

I feel my phone start to vibrate next to me. *Why is my manager calling at 7:30 on a Thursday night?* I take a deep breath and try to sound happy when I answer the phone, pretending that I wasn't just planning the funeral of my childhood dream.

"Hey Mario, what's up?"

"Avalon, you will never believe the phone call I just got."

"Alright, I'm listening." I lean forward, instantly intrigued by the fact that he could actually have good news for once.

"Well, remember how we sent your audition in for that movie a few days ago?"

"I booked it?!"

"Well, not exactly."

I let a small huff escape. "Okay? Then what's the big news?"

"Someone else saw the tape, and they would like you to meet with us tomorrow for a different job."

"What kind of other job?"

"They can't tell me over the phone; they wanted to discuss it in person."

"Mario, this sounds sketchy."

"I know, but if you knew who this came from, you would understand why."

I let out a small sigh followed by an eye roll. "Do I at least get to know who it's from?"

"No, not until tomorrow." *You're kidding, right?*

"Okay, I trust you," I say, annoyed with my manager, who somehow always gets me into situations like this, which should probably have been a red flag when signing on with him, but I was blinded by the fact that someone actually wanted to sign me.

"Great, pack a bag for two or three days, in case this goes well. The car will be there within the hour!"

"Within the hour? You said the meeting was tomorrow!"

"Yeah, but the meeting is early, and they want you to stay closer so that pick up will be easier in the morning. I think we can both agree that no one wants to come pick you up at 4:30 a.m. from that part of town."

I feel myself start to pout, knowing he's right. "Mario, I do not have the money for this. Where am I going to stay?"

"Don't worry about it. His manager booked you a room. The car will be there and take you to the hotel."

I rest my forehead against my hand, trying to fend off the stress migraine this man is going to give me. "Okay," I say, hanging up the phone and packing a bag for several nights.

The car shows up a little while later. I get in and see Mario sitting there, waiting for me with a file in his hands.

"Do I get to know anything more now?"

"No, not really. I'll be at the hotel too, right next door. We leave for the meeting at 6 a.m. They want to make sure you are there before anyone gets tipped off that he is heading into town."

"Who am I meeting?" I ask as my stomach starts to knot. Mario's words seem to echo in my ears. *Before anyone gets tipped off? Who is this guy?*

"I wish I could tell you, but that's part of the agreement. They need to make sure you can keep your cool."

"Great, so it's someone I need to keep my cool with. Another stuck-up actor," I mumble under my breath. I don't think he hears me because the rest of the ride is pretty silent.

We get to the hotel, where private security is waiting to escort me to my room. They are dressed casually to try to blend in, but it's still easy to pick them out. We get to the elevator, and I feel myself finally relax.

What am I doing? I take a deep breath, trying to wrap my head around the absurdity of this situation. *Who would want to meet with me?* I walk into my hotel room before collapsing on my bed, which is much more comfortable than the pull-out couch I've been sleeping on at home.

I set my alarm and plug in my phone. Since I am already in sweatpants, I change my shirt to a more comfortable one and go to bed. I don't know who I am meeting with tomorrow, but whatever Mario has gotten us into, I can tell it's going to be very interesting.

In the Stars • J. Karter

Chapter 3
Avalon

At 5:30 a.m., I hear my alarm go off. It was a short night, but thankfully, Mario is already texting me instructions for the day. He says to dress nice, but that there will be another outfit for me at the office if the deal goes through.

I wear a dress I've worn to a few other things and grab my makeup bag before heading out to the car. They said I would have about an hour and a half between when I get there and when they arrive, so I'll have time to get ready in the bathroom.

We pull up to a very tall building. It doesn't look like any of the agency buildings I've been to before, but every building is a little different. I've only been cast in small supporting parts as well, so maybe this is for a bigger role.

They show us the meeting room, and I walk into the bathroom to continue getting ready. When I feel as ready as I can, I walk back into the meeting room, where a woman is waiting for me.

"Hello. Are you Miss Avalon Coswell?"

"Yes, who are you?"

"My name is Aria. I will be your attendant for this morning."

"My attendant?"

"Yes, is there anything I can get you? Coffee? Breakfast of any kind?"

I hesitate for a moment. *An attendant, for me?* "Yeah, a coffee would be nice."

"Yes, ma'am. What kind?"

"What kind?"

"Yes, ma'am."

"Um, how much is this going to cost?"

"Mr. Karter has covered all the costs of this meeting. So it is of no cost to you."

Karter? Why do I know that name? "Well, in that case, can I have something that tastes like caramel?"

"Yes, of course. I will be right back with that. Do you want anything for breakfast?"

"No, just the coffee will be fine."

"Is there anything else I can get you?"

"I forgot my pen and notebook at home. Do you think you could find something for me to take notes on?"

"Of course, ma'am, I will be right back."

I watch Aria leave the room. Karter . . . Karter . . . why do I know that name? A little while later, Aria returns with my coffee and a notebook with a pen.

"Thank you, Aria."

"Of course, Miss Coswell. Is there anything else you need?"

"No, thank you, Aria." She nods and walks away. It is weird to have someone waiting on me.

As soon as I take a sip of my coffee, I hear the door open behind me. I stand up to greet whoever walks through the door. I see a man in his late forties, followed by a boy who is in his mid-twenties. We're inside, but the boy is still wearing sunglasses and a leather jacket and is carrying himself like he belongs on the cover of a magazine.

No one says anything, but no one needs to. He is immediately recognizable when he enters the room. They sit across the table from Mario and me. The older man speaks first. "Avalon Coswell,

I assume?"

"Yes, sir," I manage to choke out, shellshocked by the boy sitting in front of me.

"Avalon, this is my son, Ian Karter. I assume you have heard of him and his work?" I nod my head. I try to keep my composure while trying to deal with the fact that my brain has forgotten how to form words. I can tell by the look on Ian's face that he knows I'm starstruck.

Ian Karter, artist of the year. Number one album. Everyone knows at least one song by him. Discovered at sixteen and never looked back. *That would be why I recognize the last name.*

"Avalon, what do you know about today's meeting?" The older man asked again.

"Honestly, I don't know anything."

"Perfect," he says as he shuffles some papers in front of him. "Avalon, we would like you to date Ian."

"Yes—wait, what?"

Ian lets out a little laugh. I feel my face light up with embarrassment.

"I assume you have heard Ian's latest song."

"Of course, who hasn't?"

"Well, after the release of such an emotional piece..."

"Let's just cut to the chase," Ian interjects himself into the conversation. "I released a love song that one of my buddies wrote, and now the world expects me to have a girlfriend, and we think you would fit the part."

There's a pause before Ian speaks up again. "So, you in, princess?" he says as a smirk flickers across his face.

I sit there in shock for just a moment. My heart is pounding. My brain is running a hundred miles an hour, yet I'm still unable to process the information right in front of me. Me dating Ian Karter?

I can't tell if my stomach is filled with butterflies or in knots.

Mario looks at me. "It would be great for publicity."

"Why me?"

"Because you're a nobody." Ian says it like it's a fact. "It would be strange for me to be dating someone famous and have no one hear about it. However, dating someone like you might just be believable enough. We could pretend it just slid under the radar," Ian says, looking at me intently.

There's a pause in the conversation before his dad steps back in. "He just means that you're not a big public figure at this point in your career, and we think this arrangement could benefit both parties."

"Okay, I need some more information before I agree to anything, but I think this could work." I see a small smile creep across Ian's face as he leans back in his chair.

"Alright, let's talk details. You'll live with us at the house. There is a whole guest section of the house that will become yours. You will be given a weekly allowance for things such as phone, car, spending money, and food. Dinner will be provided on some nights when you attend an event with Ian or the family. You will also have a wardrobe allowance and a stylist for when you attend any public events. Are there any other questions?" His father says quickly as he starts to pull papers out of the envelope he carried in with him.

"Not at the moment, but I'm sure more will arise," I say as confidently as I can. I look over at Mario for reassurance.

"I had my buddy look at it last night. Everything is legit."

"So, do we have a deal?" Ian's father asks, holding out his hand.

I take a deep breath. *It's just a job.* "We have a deal."

Chapter 4
Avalon

The moment my hand touches his, I realize what I'm doing.

"Alright, I need you to sign here, here, and right over here." The lawyers are quick to jump into the conversation after I agree. Every time I sign my name, I feel like I'm signing away a piece of me. I can't tell if it's comfort or anxiety.

After feeling like I've signed my life away, I'm given my next set of instructions. "Alright, there is a stylist waiting for you outside these doors with a few dress options. You will be leaving through the back door that they are expecting Ian to leave through. You will get into the car that will then pull around front to pick up Ian."

I nod, understanding my new directions. I walk out the door and begin to face my new life. The kind of life where someone is waiting for me with a few outfits that look way out of my usual price range. My current price range is clearance at Walmart, so that's not hard to do. Still, they look amazing.

"Here, put this one on; we will figure out some more outfits once we get you home." I walk into the bathroom and put on the new outfit. When I walk out, they have a bag for my old clothes. "Here are sunglasses and a hat as well. Think of this as a *very soft launch* or a trial run for the future."

I slide the glasses on my face, hoping they cover the fear that I'm sure is surfacing behind my eyes. They lead me down some back hallways and out a back door where people with cameras are waiting. His dad tries to shield me a little bit; I'm assuming, to keep the appearance up.

We get into the car and close the door. "I think they got a few good shots. Take off the hat and make sure when Ian gets in, he has room to lean into you." I nod my head, taking off the hat and getting ready for Ian to slide into the car. When we pull up, he's signing autographs and smiling for pictures. He climbs into the car and slides close to me as the door closes.

The moment the door shuts, he slides away from me, and his smile quickly fades. The expression I am left with is something sharp and unreadable; I can't tell if it's empty or heavily guarded.

"I'll leave you two alone to get acquainted," his dad says, closing the divider between the front and the back of the car.

"So, princess. What made you take this job anyway?"

"You were in the meeting; you know as much as I do . . . actually, you probably know more. What made you choose me for the job?"

"Bold of you to assume I was the one who chose you," he says, closing the gap he had just created. I roll my eyes and slide away. "Why would you do that?" he says, leaning in and reaching for the hair that was resting on my shoulder.

"What do you want with me?" I say, leaning away from him.

"Come on, beautiful, we're supposed to be in love." Somehow his words are both sweet and emotionless at the same time. He's speaking to me like I'm fragile.

"Right now, all you're being is a creep."

He slides away. "Okay, what do we need to do to make this work?" he says, breaking an act I didn't fully realize he's been in.

"I have no idea. I haven't dated someone in forever."

"Perfect, we have a date tonight." I look at him, confused. "In the house, of course. Just a trial of a few things; see what looks most natural between the two of us."

I nod my head, my heart racing. I don't know if it's from all the camera flashes or if it's because it's just now hitting me that this is my life.

"It starts at six, don't be late. Also, wear something nice. I mean, I'm pretty sure anything would look good on you, though, so don't worry about it too much." He winks at me as I feel a shiver down my spine. I can't tell if I am crazy attracted to him or in utter shock and totally freaked out by him.

I watch out the window as we start to leave town. Soon after the city fades from view, and we pull up to this large gate, which I assume leads to the gated community where he lives. As we pull in, I look at the trees that line the street. As we get closer, I realize that it's not a street we're driving on; it's a driveway. We pull up to a house that has a few other buildings surrounding it.

"This is where you live?"

"It's where you live now, too." I sit there in shock as we pull up to the front door. Ian gets out of the opposite door and holds it open for me. He reaches his hand out. I take it and get out of the car.

I feel a little wobbly in the heels they gave me, but it's something I need to get used to. We walk through the front door, and he is still holding my hand. "Mom, we're home!"

I take a deep breath as we step inside. *What have I done?*

In the Stars • J. Karter

Chapter 5
Avalon

"You still live with your parents?" I say, teasing him a little bit.

"No, they live with me," he says with a smirk as a woman walks into the room.

"Hey, Cass, how was work?" she says, hugging him. His hand slips away from mine to hug his mom, but the moment he pulls away, his hand quickly returns to mine.

"It was good; this is Avalon, the girl I was telling you about."

"Oh, it's so nice to meet you." I smile politely and hug her. "Oh darling, you are quite tall, aren't you?" She looks me up and down and notices my shoes. "Ian, what is she doing in those heels?"

"How is this my fault?"

"Let me get you some fuzzy socks. Is that okay? I think they will be a little more comfortable than those shoes." I nod my head as she leaves the room. "Ian, show her to the couch, please."

"Yes, Mom!"

I turn to follow him to the couch but slip on the heels, catching myself with his shoulder. "Stupid shoes," I mumble under my breath, apparently a little too loud.

"Here," Ian says, sweeping me off my feet and carrying me to the couch.

"You know, I don't think this is how relationships typically start." I notice a small smile creep across his face.

"They also don't typically start with a signing of a contract and an NDA," he says as he lays me on the couch.

I sit myself up and start to unstrap my heels. I hear the door close from the backyard.

"Ian, are you home already?" I hear a male voice yell.

"Yeah, I'm in the living room," he yells.

"So no brunette? What happened?" Ian clears his throat and nods to me, undoing my shoes.

"Oh, sorry," the other boy says as I sit up, kicking off both of my heels.

"Justin, I would like you to meet Avalon."

"Dude, I know she signed on as an acting gig, but you got a girl way out of your league."

"Says the little brother living in my house and eating all my food."

"Hey, I am the supportive and lovable little brother who lives in your house and eats your food." Ian glares at him, less than amused, as their mom enters the room.

"I think these will be a little more comfortable for you," she says, handing me the fuzzy socks.

"Thank you, Mrs. Karter."

"Please, call me Grace."

"Thank you, Grace."

"You're welcome, sweetheart. Has Ian shown you to your room yet?"

"Not yet, we just got here, Mom," Ian quickly replies.

"Well, show her around and give her the tour before I do. I need more girls around here," she says with a small laugh and a wink.

"Yeah, haha. Bye, Mom," Ian says, ushering her out of the room. He turns to face Justin. "Why are you still here?" he says. His voice is laced with annoyance.

"I'm just in awe you got her to agree to this," Justin says with a slight chuckle.

"Get out," Ian says, pointing at the door.

Justin puts his hands up and walks out of the room. "I'm just saying. Out. Of. Your. League." He walks out of the room, and I hear him go upstairs.

"Well, let me give you the tour."

I take his now outstretched hand as we start walking through the house. After walking around for a while and seeing everything the house offers, we walk into another area with a closed door at the end. "This is your 'wing,'" he says with quotes.

"My wing?" I ask.

"Yeah," he says, opening the door. It's a small apartment, but it's connected to the main house. Feel free to use anything you need, but you have your own kitchen, bedroom, bathroom, and living room here."

"This is amazing," I say, in awe of the small house I now live in.

"Honestly, it's not that much; if you need anything, let me know. I will be back at six to pick you up for our date," he says with a wink. He walks out the door that connects my section to the rest of the house.

I walk towards my sliding glass door in the living room area and look out to the pool area in the backyard. I look at my stove timer, 3:30, two and a half hours until the date. I walk into my bedroom to see a walk-in closet fully stocked with clothes.

"Oh boy. This might be a little harder than I thought." I dig through the closet until I spot a light blue sundress. "Perfect," I say to myself, pulling it off the rack. I slide it off and match it with a pair of sandals.

I walk into the bathroom to find a fully stocked makeup station. "You're telling me this room has an en suite as well as a hallway bathroom? This is nicer than any place I have lived in a long time." I put the finishing touches on my makeup and use the bathroom one more time.

I take a deep breath, looking myself over in the mirror again. A faint smile tugs at my lips. I walk into the hallway just in time to hear a knock on my door. I open it to find Ian standing there.

"Ready?" he asks, holding out his arm. I take his arm as he walks me into the backyard. We sit down at a table set up in the backyard.

"So, do you like sundresses?" Ian asks, staring a little too far down, if you get what I mean.

"This has a high neckline; what could you possibly be looking at?" I ask him.

"Sorry," he says quickly, clearing his throat, trying to cover for the fact that his eyes wanted to linger for a moment longer. "That dress looks good on you."

"Thank you for the compliment. Now stop." His eyes come back up to mine with a little fake smile and a small forced laugh. "Does your mom know?"

"Know what?"

"That this is a contract," I say, gesturing between him and me.

"Yeah, she knows." There was a short pause. "She knows, my dad knows, and my brothers know."

"Brothers?"

"Yeah, Justin and Austin."

"Who's Austin?"

"Austin Karter. Famous actor, ring a bell?"

"Maybe? I haven't gone and seen a movie in a while."

"Well, I have a few premieres coming up soon, so you'll get to see some then. Now on to the next thing." I watch him reach under the table.

"You know most dates are not business meetings."

"And as we established earlier, most couples are not us," he says, peaking his head back over the table. He sets a box down on the table.

"You bought me a gift?" I say, starting to feel excited. I open it to find a new iPhone. "I thought you said I was on my own for my phone?"

"Yeah, that was until I saw you still carry your iPhone 8."

"Hey, it's all paid off," I say defensively.

"Yeah, and so is this one. It's all yours, no strings attached. If this is going to work, I need to make sure you have some tech to match mine." I nod reluctantly, accepting the gift. "Give me your phone, I'll start the transfer."

I hand him my iPhone with a cracked screen and begin to see his point. He starts the transfer when Justin walks out the back door. "What do you want, Justin?" Ian says without missing a beat.

"Mom says dinner's ready. Do you want me to bring it out to you guys, or are you two going to come in?"

"We'll be right in," I say, jumping into the conversation.

"Oh, she has some spunk," he says with a laugh.

I stand up and start to walk inside. Over the course of dinner, my phone finishes transferring everything. Dinner is long and filled with meaningless conversation; thankfully, we learn we can fake it pretty well . . . and that I can't slow dance to save my life.

I walk back to my apartment and fall face-first onto my bed. My phone goes off. I glance at it and realize I'm now in a group chat with Ian, who programmed him and his whole family into my phone over dinner.

"Meet me in the kitchen at 8 a.m. for the morning meeting," reads a text from Ian's dad, whose name is apparently Johnathan. *This is definitely not what I thought today would be, and this is going to be a whole lot harder than I thought.*

In the Stars • J. Karter

Chapter 6
Avalon

I've been here for two weeks. Every weekday morning starts with an 8 a.m. morning meeting, and most of the time, I just sit there and look pretty, which is good practice for me, I guess.

It's finally time for Ian and me to go out for the first time. The press could not get enough of the pictures from that first day. We kept the attention up on Instagram with a few carefully posted stories and one post from each of us.

It's 10 a.m., and a stylist has come to prep me for my date at noon. We're going to lunch and taking a walk through the park. I know it doesn't sound too hard, but it feels like everything is descending into chaos here.

The stylist picks out my outfit and shoes. I stand there and let her stare me up and down. By the time the process is over, it's noon, and it's time to leave for lunch. Yes, it takes my stylist two hours to do the outfit, hair, and makeup.

I walk to the car outside; when I get in, I see Ian already inside. "You ready?" he asks.

"Yeah, as ready as I'll ever be." I notice him fidgeting with the bottom of his jacket. "Are you nervous?"

"No!" he snaps back quickly. "Well, maybe just a little bit. I mean, it's not every day that you introduce a new fake relationship into the world," he says with a small laugh, still messing with the bottom of his jacket.

I move his face to meet mine. "It's also not every day that you play a sold-out stadium, yet you do that."

"Yeah, but I'm good at that," he says, winking at me.

"And I'm sure we will do fine at this," I say with a smile, trying to convince myself as much as I am him.

"Hey, Avalon."

"Yeah?" I turn and look at him.

"Question. How old are you?"

I let out a small laugh at his question. "I'm twenty-one, and your question does not give me confidence that this is going to work."

"I just wanted to check; I was thinking about ordering us some wine at lunch and wanted to make sure you're legal."

"Actually, I don't drink. You can order some, but I won't have any."

"You're twenty-one and don't drink?"

"Yeah, I don't really have the desire to."

"Alright, I guess I will scratch the wine idea then," he says with a sigh.

Was that his way of trying to swoon me? I shake the idea from my head. There's a long and uncomfortable silence before we get to the diner for lunch. When we finally arrive, we get a table outside and prepare for the paparazzi to find us.

Much to our surprise, it takes them a while, so we get a semi-relaxing lunch. When they finally arrive, we go into some of our pre-discussed poses, though I'm pretty sure his hand lingers on mine a moment longer than it needs to. It's hard to tell with him—every movement feels perfectly calculated.

We pay for lunch and get into the car to head to the next location. We get to the park and walk through it, pretending not to notice all the cameras pointed straight at us. What began as a quiet walk in the park now has the soundtrack of shutters and the glow of poorly hidden camera lenses.

I now understand why Johnathan wanted to get us out in public so that we would be recognized and still be on top of people's minds. After walking through the park for a while, we return to the car and have the driver take us home. We pull back into the mansion.

"Debrief at the pool in twenty," I hear Johnathan yell from the kitchen. I walk into my apartment, change out of my clothes, and put on a swimsuit before walking to the pool to meet them for a debrief.

"So, how did you two feel this outing went?"

"I mean, people got pictures, right? That was the goal?" I say.

"Yeah, they got pictures, but were they sold on the act?"

"Sold on the act? What reason would they have not to believe us?" I say.

"What reason do they have to suspect that this relationship is real?"

Johnathan does have a point. I randomly show up one day, disappear for two weeks, and appear for lunch and a walk through the park. There is a chance some might be asking questions.

"There is a movie premiere in two days; I suggest that when you show up there, you both are madly in love."

I nod, understanding the assignment. I feel the pressure that had just left quickly return. Once Johnathan walks away, I feel myself release the breath that I had apparently been holding in.

"So, how do you suggest we pull this thing off?" Ian says, looking at me.

I look at him in disbelief. "Me? You're asking me how we pull this off?"

"Well, you're the actress, aren't you?" I take a deep breath as he starts to walk away.

"Hey Romeo, where do you think you're going?" I say, trying to playfully catch his attention. He tilts his sunglasses down and looks straight at me.

"I prefer Casanova," he says, blowing me a kiss before walking in the back door.

I run my hands through my hair and look up at the sky. I take a deep breath, thinking of ways I can make myself look more in love with a person who clearly wants nothing to do with me.

Chapter 7
Avalon

    I hear my alarm go off at 6:30 a.m., my new morning routine. I put on a running outfit and slip my hair into a ponytail. I stretch and put in my earbuds before going on my morning run. I usually run down to the gate and back a few times. I'll even do some laps around the circle to cool down if I feel like it.

    I start running down the road, feeling the wind against my face. "Hey!" I hear a muffled sound over my music. "HEY!" I look around to see a man riding a horse.

    "I'm sorry, I had my headphones in," I say, pulling my earbuds out.

    "Who are you? I don't think I've seen you around here before."

    "I'm Avalon."

    "Oh, you're the girl that Justin wouldn't shut up about."

    "Excuse me?" I say, putting my hands on my hips.

    "Oh! No. That came out a whole lot worse than I meant it to. Let me start with this. Hi, my name is Austin. I'm Justin's twin."

    "Oh, so you're the mythical Austin I've heard about."

    "Yeah, my flight got in early this morning. I figured I would get a quick ride in before everyone else got up." There's a pause before Austin shakes himself out of his thoughts, and a slight redness appears across his face. "I probably should go put her away before everyone else gets up. I want to surprise them."

    I nod my head as he rides away. *Well, that went great*, I thought before continuing my run. I get back to my apartment and hop in the shower before getting ready for the breakfast meeting. I walk into the kitchen in the main house to find Ian and his family sitting around the table having breakfast together.

"Oh, good morning, Avalon," Johnathan says. "I forgot to text you; Austin caught an early flight back to surprise us this morning, so the morning meeting is canceled. We'll meet around noon. The stylist will be here by three. Don't forget to make sure you are ready to look in love," he says with a smile before turning back to his food.

I nod my head and start to walk away. I feel Austin's eyes track me into the next room. I make it to my doorway and walk into my apartment. I make myself a small breakfast before turning on the TV. It's not something I would typically do, but I have some unexpected time on my hands.

I go to put my dish in the dishwasher when I hear a knock at my door. I walk over, assuming it is Ian or Johnathan wanting to go over something. Grace usually texts first, and Justin tends to leave me alone. It's not that we don't get along; we just don't hang out in my apartment. More often than not, we find ourselves in the music room or playing games in the rec room.

I open the door and see Austin standing outside. "Can I come in?" he asks. I pause for a second, slightly confused about why he's at my door, much less why he wants to come in.

"Yeah," I say, mustering every ounce of confidence I can. I walk into the kitchen and load the dishwasher. "Shut the door, please," I say. I hear the door close, and he comes down the hallway to the kitchen.

"Do you normally just let strangers into your apartment?" he asks.

"We live in a gated compound. The only people here are your family and the people who work here."

"And what category do you fall under, sweetheart?"

I give him a confused look. "What do you mean?"

"Which category, family or people who work here?"

"Well, since my last name isn't Karter, I guess that means people who work here," I say with a smile.

"So you wouldn't consider yourself family even though you are dating Ian?"

"What are you trying to get at?" I say, crossing my arms. "A lot of people don't consider themselves family when they are only dating someone. I mean, we've only been dating for a few weeks."

"Can I be frank with you for a minute?"

"I mean, I thought your name was Austin, but whatever you want," I say with a shrug.

"You have spent way too much time with my father," he says while making his way over to my couch. "How does this whole relationship between you and Ian work?" he asks, kicking his feet up on my coffee table.

"What do you mean?" I say, sitting down on the other side of the couch.

"I know it's an arrangement."

I sit there, trying to hide the shocked look that appeared on my face. "Why don't you ask your brother? I'm sure he would be more than happy to go over all the details with you."

"Let's just say Ian and I don't always play nice with one another. I think you can respect that answer, considering the relationship you have with your sister."

"Leave Auburn out of this," I say, taking a deep breath and trying to remain calm.

"Do they even know you're here?"

"I signed an NDA. No one knows I'm here," I shoot back, trying to figure out what angle he's trying to play.

"If I were Malachi, I would be worried sick. You've been here for almost a month."

"That would have required him to care about me in the first

place," I reply. It comes out more defensive than I mean it to.

Austin starts to get up, but my curiosity gets the best of me. "How do you know so much about my family anyway? I never told any of you about them." He gives me a smile before he walks out of the room. I see him turn around just in time for his eyes to meet mine.

"You didn't think you were randomly picked for this, did you?" I hear him open and close the door.

I take a deep breath and run my hands through my hair. I look outside in the backyard and see the trees that sit just beyond the fence line. This place does a good job of feeling a lot bigger than it is, but it's nothing like home.

Chapter 8
Avalon

I lie on the couch, staring up at the ceiling. Would he even care if I called him?

My relationship with both my siblings has been strained since we lost Mom and Dad. Auburn and I could never get along; from the time I came into this world, she was out to get me. The last time I talked to her was at Mom's funeral. She's married now. She has a family and a life she loves, at least, that's the way it appears on social media. I still send her kids Christmas and birthday presents; we just do better when we both get to live our own lives.

Malachi, on the other hand, was a different story. He took over the farm when Dad started to get sick and stayed there to help Mom before she passed. I told him I would come home and help him on the farm, but he told me that he would rather see me as an actress than a farmer's wife. Let's just say Malachi was never the biggest fan of my cooking, or the fact that I screamed anytime a chicken came near me. I was raised on a farm, but I was definitely not made to live on a farm.

Two weeks ago, I was planning to show up on his doorstep and hope he would let me in. Today, I don't even think I can bring myself to have a phone call with him. I unlock my phone and scroll down to his name. My thumb hovers over the call button before I lock my phone and throw it on the couch.

I walk into my bedroom and face-plant on my bed so I can scream into my pillow. I hear a knock on my front door. I open it to find my stylist outside. "Who's ready for a movie premiere?' she says, way too excited.

I gesture for her to come inside. I put on an exhausted, but polite smile, trying to cover the storm of emotions the conversation with Austin brought up.

She leads me into the spare room. I think it was designed to be a guest room at one point because it has an extra bed in it, but I have covered the bed and made it an office/storage space. My stylist likes to use the extra closet for all my formal and event dresses.

"Here, this one first," she says, handing me a midnight blue floor-length dress. The look in her eyes makes her seem like she's a little girl playing dress-up. "Ian insisted you wear a dark blue dress for the premiere today."

"Of course he did," I say with a forced smile. I slip the clothes I had been wearing off so we can get me into the gown. We slide the gown up and make sure the back is secure. We grab a pair of black heels and slide them on under the dress.

"You look beautiful; let's do your makeup, and then you will be red carpet ready," she says with a squeal.

After what feels like an hour, we finally get the makeup done to match the look. She helps me stand. I walk over to the mirror and then out the door to meet Ian at the main entrance of the house. He stands there, perfectly polished. When he glances my way, it almost takes my breath away.

"You ready to be madly in love?" he says, holding out his arm. I link my arm with his.

"Always," I say, trying to find his eyes, but they left me the moment they found me. We climb into the limo, and he sits next to me.

"So, what's the game plan for tonight anyway?"

"I mean, I thought you wanted me to act overly in love, right?"

"Yeah, but what should I be expecting from you?"

I take a deep breath, pretending that the fact that he is playing on his phone during this conversation doesn't bother me. "Well, we have to stop partway down for pictures, right?"

"Yeah." His voice is short. I can tell he's treating the conversation as more of a formality than something he's actually interested in.

"I figured I could nuzzle my face into your neck a little bit, maybe look longingly in your eyes, and if I'm lucky, maybe you'll look back at me," I say, trying to add some sass in at the last part to see if that can grab some of his attention.

"That would be a treat for you, wouldn't it?" he says sarcastically. I roll my eyes and lay my head back against the headrest. "Hey, don't ruin your hair," he says.

I take a deep breath and lean my head forward again as he puts his phone back into his pocket. As soon as we get to the premiere, someone opens the door, and he gets out. He makes his way around the back of the car and opens the door for me. He holds out his hand to steady me as I get out of the car. He smiles at me expectantly, waiting for me to take his arm.

As soon as we start to walk, he leans down and whispers in my ear, "Make sure you make it believable." I let out a small giggle and make my smile even wider, pretending he told me a secret that was just for the two of us.

We stop about halfway down, and I lay my hand across his chest for the pictures, trying to close any sort of gap that can be seen. I look up at him, and he looks down and smiles back at me. He leans his forehead down and presses it against mine. It feels natural, almost as if we had practiced a hundred times, even though this is the first time.

"Got to leave them wanting more, princess," he says with a smile.

"In your dreams," I say, smiling back at him. We pull back from one another and continue down the red carpet. We get to the end, and he looks over at me.

"I didn't feel you nuzzle into my neck?"

"You've got to leave them wanting something more, right?"

He lets go of my arm as we walk into the event. Thankfully, it's a movie premiere, so there are no cameras inside the event. We walk to our seats, and I move the armrest. "What are you doing?" Ian whispers to me.

"Making this look real," I say, sitting down and cuddling up to his chest. I lay my hand on his chest and feel his heart rate faster than it was earlier in the night. "What, did I do something to make you nervous?" I say, teasing him a little bit. I feel a smile creep across my face as one also creeps across his.

"In your dreams," he replies. I look over at him and see a twinkle in his eye, and a single butterfly appears in my stomach. We watch the movie and get in the car to go home.

Of course, Ian has to do a little bit of networking, but at this point, we've practiced that so much that it feels like second nature. The car takes us back to the house, and we walk through the front door, where Johnathan is waiting for us. "So, how do you guys feel like tonight went?"

"Perfect," Ian says, moving his arm behind my back and bringing me in front of him. I spin to face him, leaving one leg behind and the other in front of him. "We've never been more in love," he says, looking deep into my eyes.

I feel my breath catch. This time, when my eyes meet his, it does take my breath away.

"I watched the red carpet," Johnathan says. I swing my leg back around so I am facing forward once again, and Ian removes his hand from my back. "If I didn't know, I would have no idea," he says with a smile. I feel relief wash over my body. "Take the weekend off. We'll meet Monday morning," he says, walking away.

I turn to look at Ian, but he's already halfway across the room, his mind moving to the next thing. "See you Monday," he calls over his shoulder, walking in the direction of the stairs.

In the Stars • J. Karter

    I walk across the house and back into my apartment. I slide off my dress and get into sweats and a t-shirt, pulling the ice cream out of my freezer. I curl up on my couch and turn on the TV. I lie there trying to use whatever media necessary to rid my brain of a lingering question. *If I called Malachi, would he even pick up?*

In the Stars • J. Karter

Chapter 9
Austin

"Well, that could not have gone worse," I whisper to myself as I pull the door to Avalon's apartment behind me.

I walk through the great room, which I still don't understand the purpose of, and start heading for the living room. We never use it unless we have company over, and even then, all of us boys try to sneak into the living room and avoid the long, drowning conversations that take place in the great room.

I jump over the back of the couch and grab the remote to turn on the TV. Justin was not lying when he talked about how gorgeous she was. I had seen some pictures from Ian stalking her Instagram before I left to go do some re-shoots just over a month ago, but her Instagram does not compare to what she really looks like.

"Speechless, am I right?" Justin says, sitting down on the ground in front of me.

"I mean, I had my doubts, but she is beautiful."

"She's also off limits; I'd like you to remember that."

"Hey, you were the one calling me and telling me how beautiful she is."

"Yeah, but we know I would never do something to hurt her and Ian, and by the look in your eye, I'm not sure the same can be said for you right now."

"What's the deal with their little arrangement anyway?"

"Why does it matter?"

"Justin, come on, I know you know the agreement. Just tell me. It would be awkward to have this conversation with Ian."

"Again, I ask, why does it matter? You're not starting a relationship with her."

"I just want to know if the option is open."

"And I'm telling you it's not."

"Have you ever thought to ask him if it was?"

"No, I haven't. Because I'm not the kind of trash who tries to steal his brother's girl."

"That's a little harsh, don't you think?"

"No, not really. Avalon is off limits; that's all you need to know about their agreement."

I feel a smirk go across my face. "You seem awfully defensive about this. I mean, Ian shouldn't be worried about anything if he's treating her right. Right? You wouldn't be worried about it if you didn't think there was some truth to the fact that I could actually steal her from him."

"Austin, I just really don't want to do this again."

"Last time I checked, Avalon and Audrey are two different girls, and Audrey was never on contract to date Ian. I mean, even if I did start to try to woo Avalon a little bit, she would still be contractually bound to Ian and whatever agreement they have. No harm, right?"

"You understand how messed up this is, right?"

"How messed up what is?" Ian asks, walking into the room.

"Ian, just the person I wanted to see."

"That's never a good sign."

"Oh, especially this time," Justin adds.

"What did you do?"

"It's not what he did; it's what he wants to do."

"Justin, he can answer for himself," Ian says as Justin stands up and gets ready to walk out of the room, stopping just at the door frame.

"Actually, I want to make sure Ian doesn't murder you." I can feel Ian glare over at Justin without even looking.

"Well, what's the question?" Ian asks, starting to get preemptively angry.

"How does this agreement you have with Avalon work exactly?"

"Why does it matter?"

"Because I think she deserves to have a guy who can take care of her."

"What is that supposed to mean?"

"I just want to make sure Avalon is happy, that's all. I mean, you do want Avalon to be happy, don't you?"

"Of course, I want Avalon to be happy. What are you getting at?"

"I mean, I've seen the way you look at her, and I can already tell that you want nothing but the best for her. But you've never seen the way she looks at me." Ian leans back off the couch and crosses his arms. "I know the way she looks at you, and you're a paycheck for her. She's contractually obligated to love you, or at least to look like she does out in public."

"Get to the point," Ian says sharply.

"All I'm saying is, it wouldn't hurt anything if she saw me behind closed doors. I just talked to her in her apartment, and I think I could see myself having a future with her. There is just this connection, you know."

"Is it the same connection you've had with the last six girls? Because that's not a connection, it's called treating girls like a conquest," Justin interjects.

"No, of course not. I would never do anything to hurt Avalon."

"Why do I struggle to believe that?" Ian says.

"Probably because we haven't met the past three girls," Justin adds.

"Guys, trust me, I've changed."

"No, I'm good," Justin says.

"Ian believes me, doesn't he?"

"No, I don't."

"You want Avalon to be happy, though, don't you? And we both know deep down that you will never be able to make her happy . . . not like I can."

"Austin, too far," Justin says, inching closer to the conversation to make sure nothing happens.

"I'm not going to fight with you about this," Ian states.

"I thought you said you wanted Avalon to be happy."

"She's happy with me."

"That's not what she just told me." I see the hurt flash across his face the moment the words leave my mouth, his normal confidence suddenly slipping away. Even if only for a moment. I feel the corner of my mouth twitch up a little bit and watch as Ian tries to regain his thoughts.

"What?"

"That's not what she told me in the apartment."

There' a long pause. Ian takes a deep breath and stares straight at me. His voice is slow and steady. "And why should I believe you? It's not like you've never lied to me before."

"What do I have to lose?" There's a stare-down between Ian and me. He's trying to find the flaw in what I'm saying. Trying to identify something he knows is a lie. I just need to sit here knowing I can pull even more information out of thin air to make my story more believable. "What if we had a little competition?" I say, trying to have some fun with the situation.

"A girl's heart is not a game."

"Then you should have no problem with me winning," I say as

Ian stands there silently. I can't tell if he is so upset he won't speak or if he is speechless. "Just don't cry when you lose . . . again," I add, slightly afraid that I might have gone too far.

"And don't be mad when you come home and your key doesn't work," Ian finally says.

"I think you're forgetting that we bought the house together?" I say, my voice sounding like a smug grin.

"No, I think you're forgetting that I bought you out with my share of the Kentucky house."

"That's right; I wonder why you'd want to sell your share of our childhood home," I say with a smirk.

"It will always be a mystery," Ian says as he walks out of the room a lot calmer than I originally anticipated.

"Why?" Justin says.

"Why what?"

"Why would you do that?"

"Because I want to give Avalon a decent shot. I think it could work."

"At the expense of your relationship with Ian?"

"Ian and I always but heads; it's what we do. We make up in the end."

"Yeah, for now."

"What is that supposed to mean?"

"Next time you see Nathan, say hi to him for me." Justin turns around and walks out of the room.

In the Stars • J. Karter

Chapter 10
Avalon

Day off. What really is a day off when you can't leave your house? I get up around 8 a.m. for my run because I might as well sleep in if I have the day off.

I finish my run and decide to go tan in the backyard while I read a book next to the pool. I grab a book off my bookshelf and go into the backyard. The moment I step outside, I hear a familiar voice.

"So, Justin tells me that Dad gave you the day off." *Austin.*

"Yeah, he did," I say, tucking my book under my arm. I walk over to the edge of the pool and lie on one of the pool chairs.

"I think we got off on the wrong foot yesterday."

"You think?" I say, turning towards him.

"Okay, I know we got off on the wrong foot yesterday. Will you give me another chance?"

"Hmm, let me think about that. No," I say before getting comfortable to read my book.

"Alright, I know I messed up. What do I need to do to earn a second chance?"

"I already told you no second chance."

"No, you said you wouldn't give me one. I'm asking what I can do to earn one."

"I don't think second chances can be earned."

"That's because you've never met me."

I sit up and face him in the pool. "And how, in your expertise, does someone earn a second chance?"

He climbs out of the pool and starts walking towards me. "Well, sometimes they can be earned by favors to one another, or by proving that you know one another." He slides the pool chair closer and sits down on it. "Another way can be proving that you want this, showing how invested you truly are," he says, leaning in a little closer. I feel his voice start to get softer. "And sometimes second chances are given because you feel a spark and you want to see where this could go."

We're now facing one another and looking into each other's eyes. "And which do you expect me to do?" I say just above a whisper. "For you?"

There's a short pause. I see a smirk cross his face. "I guess I should say for me and you, I think you're just going to forgive me and give me a second chance," he says, sitting up.

"Why would I do that?"

"Because if you didn't feel the spark between the two of us, you wouldn't have let me take your hand." He raises our hands up, my fingers intertwined with his. I feel my heart begin to race. I didn't even notice when he took it. I feel a flicker of surprise cross my face. They fit together perfectly.

"So, beautiful, what do you say?" I feel him start to slowly trace circles with his thumb on the back of my hand. I realize that even though he pointed it out, neither of us moved away. If anything, we got closer. My breath catches. "

Yeah," I say, my words barely louder than a whisper. "I think I feel it too."

He kisses the back of my hand before releasing it back to me. "Do I get a second chance?"

"Yeah."

"Perfect," he says, standing up. He spins around. "Hey, I didn't see you there. My name is Austin. I don't think I've seen you around here before?"

"I'm Avalon; it's nice to meet you, Austin." I feel a grin start to creep across my face.

"Well, Avalon, you are gorgeous. I don't know if anyone has told you that today, but I just felt like you needed to know."

"You don't look too bad yourself," I say with a smile that I can no longer hide.

"Well, thank you, Miss Avalon. If I can face the fear of being a little too bold, a little too fast, I was wondering what your plans were for tonight?"

"I don't know how my boyfriend would feel about that," I say, raising my eyebrows.

"You know there's no harm in just hanging out. What do you say?"

"Okay," I giggle.

"I'll be at your place at six," he says with a wink.

"Bold of you to think I would let a guy come in on a first date."

"Bold of you to assume I was ever planning on coming in," he says as he starts to walk away. "Besides, it's not a date; we're just hanging out, remember?" he says with a wink as he makes his way over to the back door.

I see him pause for a second before he turns around and starts speed-walking back to me. "Okay, pretend I didn't do the totally hot dramatic walk-off just yet; I forgot to ask you for your number."

He hands me his phone, and I put my number in. "I'll text you when I get inside," he whispers. "I'll be at your place at 6," he says, winking again.

I try my best to contain my laughter as he dramatically struts away. I lie back down and try to read my book one more time. I open to the first page before I feel my phone vibrate. "This is Austin."

The smile appears on my face once more, only for it to fade when I have the realization that I am falling for the brother of the guy I'm supposed to be in love with.

In the Stars • J. Karter

Chapter 11
Avalon

I know this sounds absolutely crazy to say, but even with a whole closet full of clothes, I still feel like I have nothing to wear.

I swear, Austin is just as anxious as I am because he is texting me an hour-by-hour countdown. I scour my closet and try to find something I feel comfortable in. I find a black cold-shoulder halter that had been pushed up against the wall. "Perfect," I whisper to myself as I go to grab a pair of jeans.

I put on the outfit and very light makeup and check myself in the mirror one last time. For the first time since I got here, I recognize the girl staring back at me. I hear a knock on my front door that leads to the driveway. I open it to see Austin standing there. He's wearing black jeans and a black button-down shirt.

"Dang girl, you make me feel underdressed," he says with a small laugh. He hands me the bouquet he got me.

"Hang on, let me put these in water. Do you want to come in?"

He leans up against the doorframe. "I thought you didn't let guys in on the first date?" he says with a smirk.

"Well, this isn't a date, remember." He smiles at me. I put the flowers in water and set them on the table.

He holds out his hand. "Are you ready?" I nod my head as I walk over and take it, his arm resting gently against mine. He leads me to his car. He opens my door and helps me get inside, then walks around to the driver's side and gets in. We start driving to the gate. He opens the gate and pulls out on the road.

"What are you doing?" I say, feeling a slight panic.

"Taking you out, remember?"

"Yeah, but what if we get caught?"

"Let me worry about that. You just need to worry about having fun."

I look out the window but can't seem to enjoy the scenery. I wouldn't be worried, but something in the back of my head continues to tell me that this is wrong, even though my heart keeps telling me it feels right. *Is this what it feels like to be seen?*

"As much as I love your eyes, you're gonna need these." He holds out some sunglasses. I reach for them, but he pulls them away. "Wait, give me one more look." He looks deep into my eyes and then hands me the sunglasses.

"So, do you not use a driver?" I ask, sliding the glasses on.

"Not often. Drivers are more Ian's thing than mine. I don't see the point in paying someone to drive me when I can drive myself. Don't get me wrong, there are times when I still use one, but not as often as he does." There's a short pause. "Is that okay?"

"Yeah, it's just not what I was expecting."

"Is that a good thing or a bad thing?" he asks with a chuckle.

"It's a good thing," I reply with a smile.

He reaches over and grabs my hand. "What do you want to listen to?"

"I'm okay with anything."

"No, I didn't ask what you were okay with listening to; I asked what you wanted to listen to."

"How about we hear some of your music?"

"Now, you're just trying to flatter me," he smirks, "but I guess I could oblige." He removes his hand from mine and puts some music on. His hand quickly finds its way back to mine. We drive for a while down the road while Austin gives me a private concert with his favorite playlist, plus whatever Spotify decides to randomly add in.

He pulls over on the side of the road just before we start getting into town. "Here comes the not-so-fun part."

"Okay, I don't think you can break up with me if we're only hanging out. Also, I was just kidding about not liking that song; you sounded absolutely amazing." I try to backpedal as quickly as I can, not knowing what I said wrong.

"Avalon, it's okay. I don't like that song either. What I mean is, we have to cover up part of your outfit." He reaches into the backseat and pulls out a hoodie and a baseball cap. "Put on the hoodie and put the hood on top of the hat."

I nod my head, put everything on, and situate myself again. "Even with a hoodie, hat, and sunglasses on, you are still absolutely stunning." He gets back on the road and grabs my hand once more. I look over at him. "What? My hand was getting cold," he says so innocently.

We pull into a drive-through on the edge of town. "What do you want?"

"Do they have chicken nuggets?"

"Yes, of course they do." He shakes his head, trying to hide his smile. Once we get our food, we drive to a little overlook outside of town. He parks the car and gets out. "You can undisguise yourself now if you'd like. This is Ethan's property, so no one should bother us while we're out here."

"Ethan?"

"Yeah, do you not know Ethan?" he asks, taking his hat back from me.

"No, I don't think so. Side note: I am slightly sad about giving this hoodie back."

"Then don't," he says, getting the food out of the bag.

"What?"

"Why don't you hang on to it for a bit?" I snuggle into the hoodie as he hands me my food. "So, since I'm guessing you know a bit about my family. Why don't you tell me about yours?"

"I thought you knew all about my family?"

"I looked at your Instagram. It's not too hard to get that information off of there."

"Well, I have two older siblings. Auburn is the oldest, then Malachi, then me. Dad passed when I was seventeen, and Mom passed two years ago."

Austin freezes. His face goes through a mix of compassion, heartbreak, and confusion all in a single second. "Avalon, I'm so sorry."

"It's okay. It happened." He sits there in silence for a moment, unsure of how to respond. "I don't talk to Auburn anymore, and I haven't talked to Malachi in forever," I say with a small chuckle. "I grew up on a small farm in Kansas."

"You grew up on a farm?"

"Yeah, a little shocking, right? What about you?"

"You can learn anything you want about me from a quick Google search."

"Yeah, but I'd rather ask the source."

"Well, I am a middle child. Ian is two years older than me, and Justin is fifteen minutes younger. We were all born in Kentucky and have a ranch out there. Technically, it's my ranch now, but I rent it to my cousins. Anyway, we moved to California when I was fourteen so Ian could pursue his music. I started acting, and well, eight years later, here we are."

I look over at him only to realize that he's watching me. "What?" I ask, noticing the smile across his face and the gleam in his eyes.

"Did you know you kick your feet when you eat food?"

I feel my face turn a shade of light red. "I'm sorry, was I moving the car?"

"No. No, don't be sorry, it was just adorable." He pauses. It looks as if he's trying to memorize everything about this moment. "It's perfect." He says in a whisper. We both pause as time stops. He clears his throat. "Anyway," he stutters for a moment, "what is your favorite color?"

"Wow, very original question. But it's red. What about you? What's your favorite color?" I say playfully, mocking him.

"Gold, but not just the color gold, like the gold you find when looking at something that sparkles, the kind that immediately catches your eye, no matter what color it's paired with." He looks at me with a playful gleam in his eye. "You said you grew up on a farm, right?"

"Yeah?"

"Do you, by chance, know how to ride a horse?"

"Knowing how to do something and being good at something are two different things. You know that, right?"

"Yes."

"Then yes, I know how to ride a horse. Am I good at it? Absolutely not."

He smiles at me. "I think I have an idea," he says as he walks over, helps me off the front of his car, and opens the door for me again. Once I am safely inside, he goes and gets in. "How much do you trust me?"

In the Stars • J. Karter

Chapter 12
Avalon

We pull back onto the main road and start heading to the compound. Once we get back, he parks his car in the garage, walks over, and opens my door for me.

I get out, and he grabs my hand. "Follow me," he says as he starts running, still holding onto my hand. We sprint across the lawn hand in hand until we get to the stable, and he lets go of my hand. He looks at me with a sparkle in his eye, grabs a blanket, and lays it on the horse's back. I cautiously walk up to him and the horse.

"This is Dusty. I brought him with me from Kentucky."

I look at the horse. He doesn't look as scary as the ones I remember from when I was little. We got rid of a lot of the bigger animals when I was around ten. None of us was interested in riding, and Dad really didn't have a use for them compared to what they cost us.

"Are you ready, Avalon?" Austin says, looking down at me from the horse he is now sitting on. "Do you trust me?" he asks, looking expectantly. I walk over to the block and get on the horse. It's been so long since I've been on one that it feels foreign. Yet at the same time, there's something familiar about it.

"Hold on," he says as the horse starts to move forward.

I feel my grip tighten around him. We leave the compound once more and start going down the street. We turn off just past the edge of the compound and ride through an open field. The sun is setting behind the hill in front of us. The horse walks around the edge of the hill just in time for us to see the sun start to fade behind an open field. The sky is painted shades of red and pink, making the field look as if there's a fire hidden just behind it.

"How did you find this place?" I say in awe of the scene in front of me.

"It almost reminds you of home, right?"

"Yeah, it does." I take a deep breath. "I didn't realize I missed this part."

"This was always my favorite thing to do. Sit and watch a sunset, no big city, no deadlines, no pressure, just peace."

I sit there holding onto Austin, and it feels like time stops. I lay my chest against his back and feel his steady breathing. In this moment, nothing else matters. In this moment, my jumbled mess of emotions and thoughts comes to a halt. All that matters is us and a sunset.

Then as fast as time stops, it starts back up again. We watch the last bit of the sun fade over the horizon, so only the soft glow of the sky is left to guide us home.

Austin leads the horse back home, and we both get off. "Stay right here; I'm gonna put him away, then I'll walk you home," he says with a smile.

"I live right there; you can literally see my front door from where we are."

"I know, but that's not how this works. A guy doesn't just drop you off on the sidewalk and leave. He walks you back to your front door."

I smile and wait for him by the door. He walks over a little while later and takes my hand. "You know, I really like your hands," he says with a smile.

"My hands?" I ask, confused.

"Yeah. It was supposed to sound much smoother than it did,

but I like how they fit with mine. I mean, you know, sometimes you hold hands with someone, and it doesn't feel right, or it's just awkward, and now I'm overexplaining and just need to shut up before I make anything more awkward than it already is."

He zips his mouth shut and throws away the key. I can't stop the small laugh that escapes. "I had fun tonight," I say as we approach the door.

"I did, too," he says, acting very unsure how to end this night. "Is it alright that I want to do this again?" he asks, staring into my eyes. I feel his grip on my hands get tighter.

"What do you mean?"

"Is it alright if I tell you I want to watch the sunset with you again?"

"Yeah, but I think you just want me to hold on to you again."

"Hey, a guy can have secondary motives."

I start to laugh. "Oh, I guess I should give this back to you now." I slide the hoodie off and hand it back to him. There's a long pause. "Goodnight," I say, opening my door and stepping inside.

"Goodnight," I hear him say before he walks away. I sit down on my couch—a very anticlimactic way to end the night. I turn on the TV and pull up my blanket just in time to hear a knock on my front door. I open the door and am greeted by an unexpected face.

"Justin, what are you doing here?" He stands there silently bouncing on his heels. He keeps looking at me like there's something he wants to say, but he can't find the words. "Do you want to come in?"

He nods his head as he walks through the door. "He did end up going with the carnations," Justin says, pointing to the flowers sitting on my table.

"Who did what now?" I ask, confused.

"Austin. He got the carnations for your date tonight. He was going back and forth between carnations and roses, but he thought that roses might be a little too forward."

"Austin and I weren't on a date; we were just hanging out."

"Okay, you can tell yourself whatever you want to, but when me and you hang out, you don't look like that," he says, pausing to gesture to the outfit I was wearing before returning to his sporadic pattern of pacing. "I told Austin the roses wouldn't freak you out. I mean, it's a bold gesture but not inappropriate."

"Justin, not to be rude, but why are you here?"

"What have they told you?"

"That is the broadest question I have ever heard in my life."

He lets out a sigh and narrows his lips. He pauses, carefully trying to phrase his next question. "What has Ian told you about his new song?"

"He bought it from a friend, and that landed us here," I say as he lets out a sigh. "What does that have to do with anything?" I ask, confused and slightly concerned by Justin's behavior.

"A lot more than you might think."

"Care to elaborate?"

"Do you fancy a late-night drive?"

"No, I don't. I already have confusing feelings for two brothers. I'm not adding a third to the mix."

"So you do admit that you have feelings for Austin!"

"Justin, focus! What is going on?"

"I . . . I . . . I don't think I can tell you."

"Then why are you here?"

"Because part of me hoped that you already knew."

"Is this something that is going to cause issues?"

"Immediately? Probably not. In the future, there's a good chance that if they don't come clean, we are going to be in a big mess."

"Who's they?"

"Ian and Austin."

"Who do they need to come clean to?"

"Austin needs to come clean to Ian, and Ian needs to come clean to you."

In the Stars • J. Karter

Chapter 13
Avalon

It's been six weeks—six weeks of sneaking around, six weeks of falling in love, and six weeks of secrets. "Good morning, my Starlight," Austin says, sneaking through the back door of my apartment. He wraps his arms around me and lays his head on my shoulder.

"You know my apartment connects to your house."

"I know, but it's so much more fun to sneak around." I can't help but smile when he's around. "So, did you call Malachi last night? I know you were thinking about it, but you never told me if you decided to or not?" he says, stealing some of the breakfast I've been cooking for myself.

"No, it's been two months; if he wanted to hear from me, he would have called at this point, right?"

"Yeah, but at the same time, you want to talk to him, and you haven't done anything to reach out to him."

"I guess." I feel my smile waver.

"Hey, let's change to a happier topic. Your birthday is coming up in a few days. What do you want to do for your birthday?" His arms circle around me as he starts to sway me back and forth.

"I probably have to work that night. Just because you and I both know it's my birthday doesn't mean that your dad or Ian will remember."

He spins me to face him and touches his forehead to mine. "I could always remind them, see if they'll give you the night off."

"It depends on whether there's an event that night or not."

"It's not every day that you turn twenty-two. Maybe they would give you the night off even if there was an event."

"I'm gonna say doubtful," I say as he kisses me on the forehead. "I mean, if you want to go all out, we might as well just fire up the private jet and fly to Bora Bora for the weekend."

"Getting a pilot on such short notice might be hard, but I think I can throw something together."

"I was kidding, babe." I pat his chest as I walk past with my cup of coffee.

"If it's what you want, though."

"It's not. Birthdays aren't a big thing for me. I'll just go to work like any normal day. Maybe the two of us can do cake or something this weekend? Sound good?"

"Perfect," he says, glancing at the stove clock. "Shoot, I've got to get back in there for breakfast. You're beautiful, my Starlight," he says as he walks out the back door.

"Remind me to explain to you why that is not an actual nickname."

"*Au contraire mon amour.*"

"How so?"

"How many syllables does your name have?"

"Three?"

"And how many does Starlight have?"

"Two?"

"Less syllables; therefore, it can be a nickname."

"That's not how it works."

"Then how does it work?"

"I don't know, but I know it's not like that."

"I don't make the rules; I just follow them," he says with a smirk, closing the door.

I change into a different outfit and walk through the side door and into the dining room for the morning meeting. Ian and I have been keeping all of the headlines and all of the eyes focused on us.

"Okay, so game plan this week," Ian's dad begins. "We have Instagram posts planned for Monday, Thursday, and Friday. We have a date planned for Wednesday and an awards show on Thursday. The Friday post does need to feature information from the awards show."

I nod while glancing over at Austin. Thursday is my birthday, but I know there's no way to get the day off. We set up some time to practice for interviews and what I am supposed to do during them.

"The event coordinator called today, and Austin is seated at the same table for the event. Did you ever find a date for that?" Ian's dad asks.

"Nope, I kinda like being a lone wolf. Besides, it's not your business; you're not my manager."

"But I am your father."

"But my father would respect my decision not to date," he says, looking back and forth between Ian and Johnathan.

"Everyone is free to go. Austin, come talk to me in the living room for a minute."

I watch them walk into the living room, and Justin grabs my arm. "Here, I want to show you something quick." I nod, not wanting to leave that conversation. We walk upstairs to where the boys' rooms are. "Have I ever shown you the view from the spare room? Personally, it's one of my favorites."

I follow him in, and he sits down on the ground. I start to open my mouth, and he puts one finger over his lips. He pats the ground next to him, and I sit down. He taps his ear. I hear Johnathan and Austin having a conversation in the room below.

"The vents are connected," he mouths to me as I nod. I hear a glass get set down on a table.

"Did you ever find that new manager?"

"Dad, I told you I don't drink. Besides, it's like 9 a.m. For your information, yes, I did find someone to take care of all that for me."

"They probably charge you an arm and a leg."

"Cheaper than the therapy you would cost me."

"Austin, I don't understand what I did to you."

"Dad, it's not what you did; it's what you didn't do. It's the fact you are so focused on Ian and don't care about anyone else in this house."

"I know everything that goes on in this house!"

"It's Avalon's birthday on Thursday. Did you know that?"

"Why would I care? She's not a part of this house; she's help."

"She's a person, not a pawn in a game. Does it not bother you that it has been two months, and people think Avalon and Ian are still in love? Does it not bother you that they have to put on a show every time they leave the house? Or the fact she doesn't leave the house without him?"

"Why would she need to leave the compound?"

"Because she's a person! Not property!"

"She signed the contract. She knew what she was doing."

"Did she?"

"Nathan, I mean Austin, this conversation is over."

"Mixed up one *disowned* son for another."

"You cannot talk to me like that in my house!"

"It's my house, Dad. Ian and I bought it. We let you live here. Remember whose roof you are actually under," Austin says in a tone that's firm, but calm. There's a short pause before Austin speaks up again. "Also, the conversation about Avalon is far from over."

"Respect your elders."

"Respect is a two-way street."

I look over at Justin, whose attention is moving to something else—the footsteps we hear heading down the hall. "How much do you trust me?"

"What?"

"Quick, how much do you trust me?" he forcefully whispers.

"A lot, I guess?"

"Great," he says and pushes me into the closet. "Don't say a word," he says, closing the door. I hear the footsteps get closer before stopping just outside the room. "What are you doing in Nate's room?"

"Um, just missing him a little bit extra today, I guess." I look through the slats and watch Ian step into the room, closing the door behind him. "How long before you tell Dad that you're the one managing Austin now?"

"Around the same time that you tell him about the song."

"So when you have a death wish," he says with a laugh.

"That sounds about right," Justin replies. "When are you gonna tell Avalon?" he asks.

Ian walks over and leans on the wall right next to the closet door. My heart is beating so loud I'm afraid it's going to give me away. "I don't know. It's kind of a big secret."

"I know, but it might make the situation make more sense to her."

"True, but at the same time, the lie we've got going right now seems to be doing its job pretty well."

"You know it might make the lie more believable if she met Ethan."

"True, but if she met him, she'd probably figure it out." There's a short pause before Ian speaks up again. "Besides, you two are not as slick as you think you are." He opens the closet door. "Hi,

Avalon," he says, peaking around the door with a smile.

"So you're not going to tell her?"

"No. Good try, though." Ian looks back and forth between the two of us. "What is this?" he says, gesturing between the two of us.

"This, nothing," Justin replies with a confused look.

"Okay, whatever you say." Ian walks back over to the door. "I mean, I wouldn't blame you two if you were sneaking around; it certainly would add some excitement around here." My eyes widen, and my stomach drops. *He knows.*

Chapter 14
Avalon

Thursday has finally come. I couldn't bring myself to tell Austin about what Ian said. I think that was Ian's way of telling me it was okay, but I have never been the best at reading him.

I'm also terrified by the fact that Ian knows. Austin and I were so careful—well, most of the time. There were a few times we slipped up, like when we would take one horse and both go for a ride, or when Johnathan couldn't find me one evening because I had left with Austin a few hours prior. Never anything big, but small pieces that could be easily added together.

I hear a knock on my door and open it to find my stylist outside. At this point, she has become my best friend. The only other female I can talk to is Grace, so just having a girl around is nice even if I can't tell her anything. "So, what's the vibe for tonight?"

"Awards show, you know this."

"Yeah, but are we feeling gold and glittery or dark and mysterious?"

"How did Ian say I was feeling today?"

"My instructions were, 'It's her birthday; she should be the star.'" I smile at the sentiment. Though it's all just an act, he knows how to add personal touches to make it still feel at least somewhat real.

"Is a purple dress too bold?"

"Always. But sometimes bold is what the occasion needs," she says with a smile. We go through the dresses and find a purple one.

After what feels like hours of hair and makeup, we are finally done. "You look gorgeous. No one will be able to keep their eyes off you."

"Thank you," I say, giving her a hug. I walk out into the entryway of Ian's house. As I stand there waiting, I feel my phone buzz. I see Austin's name light up my screen. "You look gorgeous, my Starlight." I look up and see him looking over the railing on the second floor.

I feel Ian come take my arm. I glance back at Austin once more before I walk out the door with Ian. We get in the car and start our drive. "Happy birthday, Avalon," Ian says with a smile.

"Thank you. I can't believe you remembered."

"How could I forget?" He said it like he was referring to a national holiday.

"Any special reason you chose to drive yourself? You always hire a driver."

"It just felt like a driving kind of night. You know it is a special occasion," he says, winking at me before turning into the parking lot. We get to the event and find our way inside. We pause for photos, and I lay my head on his neck.

"You smell different," I whisper in his ear.

"Yeah, it's Austin's. Thought you might enjoy it."

I feel my heart skip a beat and a chill go down my spine. We go back to walking down the red carpet. Thankfully, he doesn't get caught for too many interviews, so we make it down faster than we normally do. My stylist was right, though. No one could keep their eyes off me.

Award shows feel different to me than some other events because we are being watched the entire time. At other events we at least get to do something. At the last release party, we both got to walk around the room; at movie premieres, we watch the movie. Here, we intend to watch people win awards, but there are cameras pointed at the crowd the whole time.

Austin and Ian don't win anything, but neither of them was expecting to, so it's not too much of a shock. Ian doesn't stay to talk to anyone, so we get out of there a lot faster than normal.

"Did you not need to do any networking?"

"Na, the people here will be the same ones I see next time." We get in the car. "Besides, the night is still young, and I want to give you some time to celebrate your birthday." We start driving down the road towards home when he turns off early.

"Where are we going?"

"I want to talk to you about something." We drive down a windy road to a city overlook. "It's usually pretty quiet up here, so we shouldn't be disturbed." I nod. Ian takes a deep breath, looking at me. "I haven't been entirely honest with you, and I feel like it's time to come clean about a few things."

"Alright."

"The song that Ethan wrote. The love song I released a few weeks before we met."

"Yeah?"

"I wrote it. It's my song. No ghostwriter, no friend, my song."

"Ian, that's great, but I don't understand what that has to do with anything."

"Avalon, there's another girl."

I feel a ping in my chest. Even though I know there's nothing between us, it still hurts a little bit to hear it. "Okay, you pay me to do this, so it's not like there's an 'Us.'"

"Avalon, there's not an 'us,' but there is a You and Austin." I bite my bottom lip. "I know about you two," he says, leaning in a little bit closer. "I have a girl I can't be with. I know what it's like being in love with someone and needing to hide it deep inside. I know what it's like watching her kiss the other guy, knowing that it's something that you can never have. I can't do that to Austin."

The space between us has closed, and his voice is almost a

whisper. "Is this where you fire me?" I quietly ask.

"No," he says, leaning back. "This is where I tell you to go be with Austin. You have to keep up your end of the contract, but I don't want to be the thing that stops you and Austin from being together." I sit there in shock for a moment. "You and I will be professional. You and Austin can be personal."

"Thank you," I choke out.

"Happy birthday, Avalon," he says, backing out of the parking space and heading back home. We pull into the compound and park in the garage.

"Well, thank you," I say with a smile, "for everything."

"Of course. But you didn't think your evening was going to end there, did you?" I give him a confused look. "Oh, sweetheart," he says with a laugh.

He walks me to the back patio by the pool. The pergola has string lights hanging from the top, and there stands Austin waiting for me. Ian leaned down and whispered in my ear. "My parents are gone for the weekend. Don't worry about getting caught; just have fun."

I walk over to meet Austin under the lights. He's still in his suit from the awards show. He takes my hands and looks me in the eyes. "Can we give this a shot for real this time?"

I nod my head. "Yeah, I think I'd like that." He wraps my hands around his neck and places his hands on my back, and the portable speaker starts playing music. We dance momentarily before closing the gap between our two bodies.

His forehead meets mine before he whispers, "Can I kiss you now?"

I glance over to where Ian went into the shadows. *He's gone.* I look deeply into Austin's eyes before I lean in, and the next thing I know, his hand finds its way up my back and at the bottom of my hair. The other is still sitting behind my lower back, holding me close. We only pull away for a moment to catch our breath. "You have no idea how long I've wanted to do that," he says with a smile.

We are getting ready to lean back in when we hear a car door close. I quickly pull away, leaving only his hand still holding my face. I face the back door and see Justin walk in with someone else.

"I might have planned something for your birthday weekend before I knew this was going to work," he says, rubbing the back of his neck.

"AVVY!" I know that voice. No. It can't be. "Malachi?"

In the Stars • J. Karter

Chapter 15
Ian

I watch Avalon make her way to Austin. It's a lot more painful than I thought it would be. Audrey hasn't been in the picture for several years—eight years, to be exact. I wrote the song when I was sixteen, around the time we moved here.

I head upstairs to my room and start taking off my suit, carefully setting it aside to be dry cleaned. I see headlights pull up into the driveway, and two figures exit. "And the main event has arrived," I sigh. I guess Austin is better for her; he knows what she wants and understands her in ways that I don't.

I grab the sweatpants and t-shirt that I laid out for myself earlier in the day and change before going downstairs to see if I can still catch the reunion. I know Austin wanted to talk to her a little bit before the big reveal, so I still have time.

I wash off Austin's cologne that he let me borrow. I always hate his cologne. He always gravitates toward the ocean-type smells, while I always gravitate toward musk or wood-type scents. I grab my body wash and wash my neck off, so I at least am able to smell like myself again.

I look up at myself in the mirror, and I see a shell of myself staring back at me. "As long as she is happy," I whisper, finding the broken person hiding behind my eyes. She was never supposed to be mine; it was always temporary. *We were always temporary.*

The one month has clearly come and gone, but I don't want her to leave. I love her. I know I do, and I know I can never tell her. *She's the one I can never have, the one I have to watch be with someone else.*

I take a few deep breaths before heading downstairs. By the time I get down there, I see Malachi and Justin walking outside. I quietly sneak out the back door and hide in the shadows to watch a reunion that I can only ever hope to experience. I hide quietly in the shadows, silent and still.

She's the story I never got to tell.

Chapter 16
Avalon

He comes closer, and I can see him clearly. "Malachi!" I run and give him a hug.

"Look how grown up you look."

"Yeah, it has been a couple of years," I say in disbelief that he's standing in front of me.

"I'm Austin," he interjects himself in the conversation.

"You were the one I talked to on the phone."

"That's me."

"How did you find him?" I say, turning to look at Austin.

"Your Instagram," he says with a laugh. "Yeah, you should have seen the confusion on my face when someone with a blue check mark was trying to message me." I laugh too, knowing how he would react.

He wanted me to follow my dream of fame, but he never really wanted anything to do with it. I moved out right after high school and have been trying to make it on my own since then. Malachi was always my biggest cheerleader.

"How have you been? I've missed you so much," he says, giving me another hug, causing Austin to remove his arm from my back.

"I've been good," I say, putting a fake smile across my face.

"Hey, let me show you to your room," Justin says, leaving me alone with Austin.

"So . . . I sense I might have made a mistake." I glare at him. "I promise it was supposed to be a romantic gesture."

"What part of brother screams romance to you?"

"More like reconnecting with family?"

"Austin."

"I'm sorry; I saw how much you wanted to see him, so I talked to him and got him a flight out here so you can spend the weekend together. He leaves on Saturday afternoon, so just try to enjoy spending time with him. It's only one day."

I look into his green eyes and know he was just trying to do something sweet. "Okay," I say, grabbing onto his suit jacket. "I was just hoping you and I would get to spend some time together this weekend," I add, feeling down the lapels of his jacket.

"What do you think Saturday night is for?" he says with a wink. He kisses my forehead before walking inside to check on Justin and Malachi.

"I told him it was a bad idea." I hear Ian's voice break through the darkness on the side of the house.

"I'm not in the mood, Ian."

"You were in the mood, but Austin did a good job of killing that."

"Boundaries!" I cry. He rolls his eyes at me.

"Avvy, definitely using that nickname. I can't believe it's been two months, and I hadn't thought of that yet."

"What do you want, Ian?"

He walks over and holds out his arm. "I want to make sure you make it home safe. Even though I don't always act like it, Mamma did raise me as a country gentleman."

"What's your angle?"

"A good conversation for the next few feet." I trip as my heel falls into the dirt. "And to make sure you make it home with no broken bones," he says while catching me and helping me stand back up.

I take his arm as he starts walking me to the back door. "I know you might not have wanted to see Malachi, but I would give just about anything to have Nathan walk through that door. Even if you have to fake it, make it seem like you want him here for our sakes."

"It's not that I don't want Malachi here. It's that I wasn't expecting to have him here."

"What's wrong with having him here?"

"I haven't talked to him much since Mom died. We were close when we were kids, but we went in different directions. He doesn't know me anymore."

Ian takes a deep breath. "Yeah, I get that."

"I've been thinking about trying to call him sometime soon and see how he is, but there's a big difference between a phone call and getting on a plane to come visit someone."

"At least you know he still cares."

"Yeah."

We sit down on the chairs by my back door. "Avalon, Malachi would not have gotten on a plane and flown halfway across the country if he didn't care about you."

"So that's the definition of caring for someone, flying across the country for them."

"Avalon."

"Caring doesn't mean physical gifts or things that involve a lot of money. Caring involves consistency. It's not a one-and-done type of thing. You can't just pick when you care about someone and when you don't. I waited for months for him to call, and nothing."

I kick my shoes off and stand barefoot on my back patio, feeling the cold concrete beneath my feet as I stare off into the night, watching the wind blow through the trees on the edge of the property.

"You can't blame him for not calling if you didn't try either," Ian says softly, standing next to me.

"I got tired of trying. I am tired of being the only one who tries. If I don't text first, I won't get a text. I am tired of waiting for him to find time for a grand gesture that suddenly fixes all of our problems."

"Avalon."

"It's not my fault."

I watch as Ian's face softens and shifts to concern. "What's not your fault?"

"It's not my fault I left; it's not my fault he stopped texting; it's not my fault he had to take over the farm. He's the one who told me to leave. He can't just come and pretend like nothing happened when he missed three years of everything."

"Wait, I thought you said that you were headed back to the farm if things hadn't worked out."

"And now you see how truly desperate I was for this job." I feel my face go numb. No emotion, no feeling, just blank.

"Avalon, I understand that you can't just pretend to care for someone..."

"What do you mean? You do it to me every day," I say, feeling my heart ache the moment the words leave my lips. I look up and meet his blue eyes. I didn't realize that we had gotten so close to one another. His hands are holding onto my arms, making me face him, his eyes staring deeply into mine.

I feel my heart speed up. My breathing becomes deeper and matches his. His forehead gently rests against mine. "Who says I'm faking anything?"

He pulls his forehead away and loosens his grip on my arms. Then he takes a step back and looks at me. "Get changed; they'll be waiting for you in the living room," he says with no emotion before turning around and walking away, back into the darkness where he came from.

In the Stars • J. Karter

I open my back door and find a change of clothes, pull back my hair, and get ready to walk into the main house's living room, pretending like nothing happened.

In the Stars • J. Karter

Chapter 17
Austin

I follow Justin and Malachi into the house and quickly run upstairs to change out of the suit from the awards show into something a little bit more casual. By the time I get downstairs, I see Justin talking with Malachi on the couch and Ian finding his way back inside.

"Ian," I whisper, trying to get his attention. "Ian," I say a little louder, trying not to disrupt Justin's conversation. He turns, looks at me, rolls his eyes, and heads up the other staircase.

I start walking over to the back door when I hear Avalon's door open. I walk over to her and wrap my arms around her. "Hey, I'm sorry I didn't think about how this might make you feel."

"You know, I . . . I don't want to talk about it right now."

I brush the hair out of her face with my hand. "You look beautiful tonight." She gives me a small smile before she starts to walk away. "Avalon, look at me," I say, spinning her to face me.

"What?" she says.

I'm not sure if she's frustrated or flustered. "I'm sorry, I really am."

"I know."

"What can I do to fix this?"

"Nothing, it's fine. I'm not mad; I'm just a little caught off guard. I really wish you had asked me first." I let out a sigh. "I do appreciate the gesture, though; it's just not how I thought this night would go."

"Me either," I say with a small smile. "Why don't you go get settled? I'm going to go ask Ian if he wants to join us for a few games."

"Oh, what game?"

"No idea, they were still trying to decide when I left." She smiles at me before walking away. "Wait." I grab her hand and she turns back to face me. "One quick kiss before you go."

Her smile grows wider as she comes in close for a kiss. I let the kiss linger—not too long, but long enough to make sure it leaves a trace. Something marking me as hers, and something marking her as mine.

"I could get used to that," I say with a smile. I slowly let her hand go as she walks towards Justin and Malachi. I walk upstairs following the same path Ian took to get back to his room. I knock on his door.

"What?"

"Can I come in?"

"No."

I open his door and walk in anyway. "Did you really think saying 'no' was going to stop me from coming in?"

"Not in the slightest, but I was curious about what you were going to do. What do you want?" he asks, sitting up in his bed and setting his notebook on the nightstand beside him.

"I just wanted to ask if you wanted to join the four of us for some games downstairs."

"No thanks. I'm kinda tired. I think I'm just gonna turn in for the night."

"That's fine." I start to walk back out the door. "Oh, Ian, I almost forgot."

"Hmm," he says, looking up from the scribbled-on page of the notebook he had once again begun working on.

"I win," I say, wiping the last bit of Avalon's lipstick off my bottom lip before closing his door and heading back downstairs.

In the Stars • J. Karter

Chapter 18
Avalon

The weekend leaves as quickly as it came, and Johnathan and Grace return home first thing Monday morning, ready for the morning meeting.

"As for the event on Thursday, you two did very well on the red carpet." I feel Ian's hand come and find mine under the table.

As far as Austin and I are concerned, I don't know. After Malachi came on Thursday night and we got into that little spat, he's kind of kept his distance from me. I'm not mad at him; I just wish he had told me and had a little bit of different timing.

I zone out of the meeting and let my mind wander for a moment. I know he is going to send out meeting notes with everything I need to know anyway. It can be hard to focus, as a lot of the information tends to be irrelevant to my job.

"Avalon, dismissed," I hear Johnathan say forcefully. By the look on his face, this is not the first time he said it. I get up, leave the table, and attempt to find Austin, who was absent from breakfast this morning. I walk up to his room and knock on the door.

The door swings open by itself. I find a note on his bed addressed to me. "I'll be home in three days. Needed to go out of town for work. I found out at the last minute and didn't want to wake you."

"Apparently, leaving town doesn't warrant a text," I mumble, setting the letter back down. I pull out my phone and send him a text. "See you in three days! Miss you already!"

I type out one more message and let my finger hover over the send button. *I love you.* I delete the message and put it back in my pocket. I turn to leave and see Ian standing at the door.

"Where's Austin?"

"Out of town," I say, handing Ian the letter he left on the bed. Ian rolls his eyes. "Does he do this often?"

"What, leave for work without telling anyone? Or avoid his problems like the plague?"

"We're not having problems."

"Yeah, that's why there's a handwritten note on his bed as opposed to texting you before he left or telling you where he went." I glare at him. "Or can you not have problems in your seventy-two-hour-old relationship?" There's a pause. Ian is blocking the door, so I can't leave. "Okay, that might be a little unfair," he says, softening a bit.

"A little?"

"Oh, calm down. In all seriousness, Austin has the conflict resolution skills of a two-year-old."

"Come on, be realistic. He can talk out his emotions; that's at least four or five years old," Justin says from behind Ian. Ian lifts his arm so Justin can enter the room. "Where did he go this time?" Justin asks, picking up the note. "Oh, work thing, good excuse."

"Do you know where he is?"

"Do I know? No. If I had to guess, probably back in Kentucky. That is usually where he likes to go to run away from life."

"Was it something I did?"

"No, he'll be back in a few days and be Austin again." Ian looks at Justin, confused. Justin nods his head to the wall. Ian gets a look on his face—like everything suddenly makes sense, as if Justin had silently handed him the piece of the puzzle he had forgotten.

"Oh," Ian says, the sharpness in his voice replaced by something softer.

"Do I get to know about the unspoken communication?" I blurt out, starting to get frustrated.

Ian looks at me for a minute. "It's Nate's birthday tomorrow."

"Okay? Who's Nate?"

"Austin is leaving town for work next week, just so you guys know," Justin adds, trying to redirect the conversation.

"That doesn't have anything to do with Nate."

"Yeah, I know," he says, moving Ian's arm and walking out of the room.

"Are you going to answer my question?"

"Not this one," Ian says before walking out of the room. I walk back downstairs and into my apartment. As I close my door, I feel my phone vibrate. I glance down and see a text from Austin. "Miss you too. I'll be home soon."

I lock my phone and slide it back into my pocket. *More secrets.* That's the only thought that is echoing through my head. All that's happened since I got here is secret on top of secret, and Austin only amplifies it.

Don't get me wrong, I love Austin, or at least I think I do. I know him well enough to know something is wrong, but maybe I'm just overthinking. I try to talk myself out of all the worst-case scenarios. I don't know what I did, but I feel like it's my fault that Austin left.

I hear a knock. I walk over to see Grace standing at my glass door. I quickly invite her inside. "Come in," I say, mustering the biggest and fakest smile I can as I show her to the couch.

"My beautiful Avalon," she says as I look at her, confused. She hands me a plate of freshly baked cookies.

"To what do I owe the pleasure?" I say with a smile on my face.

"Avalon, you can cut the theatrics with me, my dear. I know everything that's going on."

I feel my heart skip a beat. "I can assure you I don't know what you're talking about," I say, trying to recover.

"I know you love him."

I let out a sigh. "Yeah, I do." I feel my facade fade.

"Please just be careful with Austin when you tell him."

"Why so?"

"This time of year is a little hard for Austin. We had some family drama a few years ago, and he got caught in the middle of some stuff. Along with his history of relationships . . ." Her voice fades. "I just want you to be careful with him, sweetheart," she says, a look of motherly concern on her face.

"Of course, Grace," I say with a soft smile. We talk for a moment more before Grace walks back to the house. I follow her over and walk upstairs to Ian's room. I open the door to find him sitting with his guitar, playing with a melody.

"Hello, can I help you?"

"I need answers," I say, walking into his room and closing the door behind me.

"And I need a shirt, but you're standing in front of my closet." I move over so he can grab one, putting it on before returning to his bed once again. "What's this urgent question?"

"What happened with Nathan?"

"Nathan, Nathan, Nathan, I'm sorry, I don't recognize that name."

"Ian."

"I wish I could help you darlin', but I don't recognize the name, Nathan."

"Nathan, your brother."

He pauses for a minute. "I don't have a brother named Nathan. Austin and Justin might, but I don't have a brother named Nathan."

"That's not how family works."

"Really, how's your sister?"

"That's not fair."

"And it's not fair for you to ask me about Nathan."

In the Stars • J. Karter

Chapter 19
Avalon

It's been two months since my birthday. True to his word, Austin came back three days later, and just like Justin had predicted, everything was fine. It was like nothing had ever happened.

Also true to Justin's word, Austin had to leave for filming the next week. He's come home once or twice when he can, but it's a lot of weird-hour texts and phone calls. I keep trying to remind myself that I knew what I was getting into when I started dating Austin, but I'm not so sure I did.

I pull myself out of my thoughts as I throw my blanket over my shoulder. I leave my apartment and pull back my hair as I walk to the morning meeting. Ian is recording something this morning, so the morning meeting was moved to 6:00 a.m. before he needs to leave for the day.

I sit down, and Ian hands me a cup of coffee. I take a sip of it and look down, confused. "Three cream, two sugar, right?" he quietly asks as Johnathan sits there fighting with his laptop, trying to turn it on.

"Yeah, but how did you know?" He shrugs his shoulders. "Thank you," I say, continuing to drink the only thing currently keeping me awake. Johnathan pulls out a folder and sets it on the table in front of Ian and me.

"Something was recently brought to my attention," Johnathan says very carefully as Ian leans back and crosses his arms. "Avalon, it has been brought to my attention that you have not been able to travel since this whole arrangement began."

I look at him, much more awake than I previously had been, and very skeptical of where this is going. I lean forward, putting my arms on the table. "It's been four months of this relationship, and I feel like the logical next step would be for you two to take a trip together."

"Trip to where?"

"Wherever you would like, Av," Ian says, sliding the folder over to me. I look over at him, waiting for him to explain the catch. "No catch," he says. I stare at him a little bit longer, knowing that something like this doesn't just happen for fun. "Except for the fact that we will have to be seen with each other for sightseeing a few times."

In the big picture, that's not actually the hardest request. We finish the meeting, and Ian pats the top of my head before heading to record for the rest of the day. I walk back to my apartment, tightly holding my blanket around my shoulders, feeling the weight of it trail behind me.

I go back to bed for a few hours. I wake up to my phone buzzing next to me. "Hello?" I say very groggily.

"Good morning, beautiful." I look at who called me—Ian.

"Hey, handsome, what's up?" I say, not knowing if someone else can hear our conversation.

"You want to come see me at work today?"

"Always."

"Great, there will be a car there in about twenty minutes. Will you bring me some lunch as well?"

"Of course, I'll see you soon, okay?"

"See you soon."

I hang up the phone and get ready in more casual clothes. I don't want to dress super nice if we are just heading to his studio, but I do want to make sure I stay picture-ready.

I see the car pull up outside and start to get in the back. "Why are you getting in the backseat?" I hear a voice from the front say. I see Justin sitting in the driver's seat.

"I thought Ian was sending me a car?"

"He did; I canceled it."

I get out of the back and get into the passenger seat. "Then you can't blame me for not knowing," I say, buckling my seat belt.

"He sent the car for both of us, but I'd rather drive my own car than have someone drive me around. If I drive myself, then I can pick when I leave; if I have a driver, I have to wait for them to pull the car around."

I nod in agreement. I never really have the choice of whether to have a driver or not since I don't have a car. I could probably afford one now, but I just haven't gotten around to it.

"Ian wants lunch," I tell Justin, just in case the message didn't get relayed to him. He pulls into a McDonald's.

"What does he want?" Justin whispers. I lean over him and yell into the loudspeaker. "Can I get a cheeseburger and fries with a Dr. Pepper, and an additional burger. No pickles. We also need a chicken nugget meal with spicy mustard and a chocolate shake."

"Anything else?" the man asks. Justin gives his order and pulls around to the window.

"If I'm driving you to him, the least he can do is get my lunch."

"I thought you were the one who dismissed the driver."

"Yeah, so? I'm still bringing his very beautiful girlfriend to him." I glare at him for a minute. "Say what you want to, but you just got out of bed to go sit in a recording studio."

"Yeah, because he called and asked me to."

"Avalon, what exactly do you think is going to happen at the recording studio?"

"I don't know; I'm guessing there's someone there I need to

meet or some sort of photo thing that we're doing," I say as Justin hands me the bag.

"Avalon, you're bringing him lunch."

"Yeah?" I say, grabbing a few of the fries.

"Avalon, Ian doesn't let anyone in the recording studio."

"Then why are you going?"

"I'm family. He usually only allows family to come in."

"Okay?" I say, unsure of where this conversation is headed.

"Avalon, do you still not get this?"

"No, apparently I don't."

"He wants you to be there and *support* him. No media, no big stunt. He just wants you there to support him."

"That doesn't make sense though."

"Why?"

There's a pause. "Not to be rude, but what part of this don't you understand?"

"He pays me to act like I'm in love with him."

Justin interrupts me before I can start another sentence. "Did it ever occur to you that no one pays him for this stunt?"

"What do you mean? He gets something from this; it's all for that song. He needed to be in a relationship for media purposes."

"Avalon, no one gives a crap about that song anymore. He's releasing new music. Everyone has moved on from the song."

"Yeah, but . . ."

"It's not about the song!"

If it's not about the song, then why am I still here? I feel the car go into park, and I get out as fast as I can.

"Avalon!"

"I'm done with this conversation," I snap back at Justin, who is just now getting out of the car.

"Do you even know where you're going?"

"No, but I'll figure it out!" I say, getting in the elevator and heading for the lobby.

In the Stars • J. Karter

Chapter 20
Avalon

I take the elevator up to the lobby and walk to the front desk, trying to think about anything other than what Justin just said.

"I'm looking for Ian Karter," I say to the woman working at the front desk.

"I'm sorry, ma'am, I can't release that information to you." I slide my sunglasses down a little bit and look over the top of them at her. "Oh, Miss Coswell. I will call up to his studio right now for approval."

I stand there as she calls up to him. I notice my foot tapping as I glance around the room, making sure Justin didn't follow me. I can hear someone on the other side of the phone as she writes some information on a piece of paper and lays it down in front of me.

"He's up on the fifth floor. Take these elevators right behind me up to the fifth floor; this is his room number." She circles the number 504. "Once you get off, you are going to head to your left, and it should be right there."

I nod and thank her before I head to the elevator. I take a deep breath when I get inside. I manage to collect myself a little bit before I walk down the hall and see Justin standing outside the door.

"It took you long enough," he says with a small laugh.

"Is he in there?" I ask.

"Avalon, I'm sorry. I shouldn't have said what I said." I stare at him, still frustrated from our conversation in the car. "He hasn't told me anything, so I don't know anything for sure. I just jumped to a conclusion based on what I've seen between the two of you, but really, whatever is going on . . ." I glare at him. "If anything is going on, it's between you two. I'm sorry for trying to insert myself into places that I shouldn't be in."

"Thank you," I say.

"Are we good?"

"Yeah, we're good," I say as the door opens, and Ian stands on the other side.

"Oh, McDonald's, my favorite." He grabs the bag from me.

"My lunch is in there, too," I say as I follow him into the room.

"No pickles?" he asks, grabbing his sandwich out of his bag.

"Yeah, that's right, isn't it?"

"Yeah, but how did you know?"

"How do you know how I like my coffee?"

"Touche." He sits down with his meal and looks at everyone who is there to help him record. "Let's take lunch. We'll restart at one."

I look at the clock, and it's just before noon. They all nod their heads and leave the room, leaving Justin, Ian, and me alone in the room. Ian walks over to the couch, grabs a blanket, and spreads it on the floor. "Fancy a picnic?"

I sit down on the blanket, and we start carefully laying out our food. "So, do you know where you want to go on our trip yet?"

"Honestly, I haven't even looked at that file yet. I went back to bed after you left," I say with a small laugh, slightly embarrassed by the lack of things I have accomplished today.

"Well, can I tell you some of my favorites? And if you want to go someplace not in the file, we can do that too," he says, eating some fries.

"Wait, what trip?" Justin interjects. Ian shoots him a look, and he quiets back down.

"What places do you enjoy?" I ask, subtly stealing some of the fries that he had set down on the blanket.

"Well, there's Florida, which is always fun. I don't know if you've been to New York, but it could be cool if you've never been there. I enjoy going into the mountains if you want to do something like that. We could also go overseas somewhere if that's something you want to do."

I stop and think about it for a moment. "Can we go to Arkansas? Or Missouri? I like the trees there, and I kinda miss the Midwest."

"Yeah, we can do that," he says with a grin. "I'll start looking at dates and flights when I get home tonight." I smile back at him. I recognize that twinkle in his eye. He's up to something. "Do you like traveling?" he asks me.

"Yeah, I guess. I haven't done a lot of it recently . . . or ever . . . but I think it's fun."

"Okay," he says, a smile now fully present on his face.

My only thought is *Ian, what are you planning?* I can't help but be mesmerized by him, his blue eyes staring deep into mine, his smile giving me butterflies. The world pauses for just a moment until Justin starts it spinning once again.

"I hate to interrupt this very interesting moment that may or may not be happening here." He looks between Ian and me before finishing his question. "But what's this about a trip?"

Ian rolls his eyes and looks back at Justin, slightly annoyed with the second interruption. "Avalon and I are going on a trip. I mean, Dad realized that Avalon has not really had the ability to travel since this whole thing started, so I am taking her on a trip wherever she wants to go." He smiles, moves next to me, and wraps his arm around my back.

"Sounds fun, do the rest of us get to come?" Justin says, looking at Ian, wanting to know if he can tag along on our little trip.

"No, Avalon and I are going on a trip. Not our family and

Avalon. Not Avalon, Ian, and Justin either. Just Ian and Avalon."

I smile up at him and feel my face start to heat up. His hand slides across my back and down my arm to find my hand.

"Here, let me show you what I've been working on." He leads me over to the computer and hits play on the track they were recording prior to us walking in. He hands me a pair of headphones.

"Ian, this sounds amazing."

"Av, you're yelling," he says, moving one ear of the headphones off.

"Sorry," I say with a little laugh and what I'm sure is a bright red face. I listen to three of his new songs before people start coming back in to help him record.

"You guys can stay if you want, or you can head home. I just need Justin to do some drum work for me before he leaves." Justin nods his head and walks into the recording area while I find a seat on the couch. Justin puts on a pair of headphones and sits down behind the drums.

Ian walks up to a microphone. "Can you do that thing you were showing me the other night in the backyard? I have the rhythm down, but I can't quite match what you had in mind." Justin nods his head, and the guy at the computer gives him a thumbs up.

I listen to him record the drum part they had just talked about. He records a few other short little things after that, then Ian tells him he's done. Justin walks out and grabs his keys off the table where he set them earlier.

"See you at home tonight?" Ian asks me, walking towards where Justin and I are, and away from the computer.

"Yeah, I'll see you tonight," I say with a smile. Ian leans down, and I get up on my toes. Our lips gently press together for what feels like just a second. We step away from one another, and he walks into the recording studio.

I wave to him as I leave the room and step out in the hallway to wait for Justin. My back is pressed against the wall, and a smile is plastered across my face. *Well, that was new.*

In the Stars • J. Karter

Chapter 21
Avalon

Justin walks out of the room. I immediately try to hide every emotion that I am feeling and trying to process in that moment.

"Ready?" he asks, tossing his keys up in the air and catching them again.

"Yeah, I'm ready," I say, my heart still pounding.

We walk to the elevator and head back to the car in the parking garage. As we climb in, I realize that I have either been so caught up in my own thoughts that I didn't hear him, or that Justin has said nothing. I feel the car back out and start heading out of the parking garage.

"So, do you want to talk about what I just saw, or would you rather we ignore it and move on with our lives?"

I let out a breath that I didn't even realize I had been holding in. "So you did see it?" I say, feeling defeated.

"Yeah, I'm pretty sure everyone in the room saw it. It wasn't the most subtle kiss in the world."

I put my head in my hands out of frustration, but also out of embarrassment. "Agh!"

"How could you possibly be upset with what just happened?"

"Because I'm not supposed to be dating Ian; I'm dating Austin."

"Yeah, but you are being paid to act like you are dating Ian. Besides, when was the last time you talked to Austin?"

"I know, I know. It's just hard."

There's a short pause. "Avalon, be honest with me. When was the last time you talked to Austin?"

"I don't see why that's relevant," I say defensively.

"Avalon, seriously. How long?" I sit there in thought for a moment, skeptical about why Justin wants to know.

"Can't you just ask Austin?" I say with a sigh.

"I'm asking you. How long?"

"Almost two weeks."

"Two weeks?" he asks, clarifying what I just said as his eyes grow wide.

"*Yeah, two weeks.*"

"Okay, first off, you don't need to feel guilty about kissing Ian. That is what you were hired to do: make it look like you two are dating, and people in relationships do kiss. Austin is aware of this; if he finds out you two kissed, he won't be shocked. Just pretend you and Ian went a little bit off-script for a minute, and it was what was best for the plot. Okay? Second off, you need to be aware that two weeks of not talking to someone you are in a relationship with is not okay."

"Okay, but that's not the rule; I mean, some people are in places without cell service or can't contact someone for two weeks." I snap just a little bit, trying to keep my temper under control. Attempting to avoid getting into a fight like we did on the way over.

"Avalon, this is not one of those situations, and you know it." I feel myself starting to pout a little bit. "Avalon, why does this make you so upset? You have been fake dating Ian for months and seeing Austin for months; what changed?"

"Nothing, everything is the same. Nothing changed." Justin pulls into a parking lot. I feel the car shift into park, and he turns his attention to me. "This isn't home; we didn't need to run any errands, did we?" I say, trying to change or at least divert the conversation.

"Avalon, look at me."

I roll my eyes, trying to hide every emotion I possibly can. Maybe if I put on a stone face, then this conversation can end without me saying anything. He turns down the radio. There's a long pause as he observes my face, looking for any sign of emotion. The car is totally silent; even the sound of the engine has faded.

"Avalon, I'm going to ask one more time. What changed?"

Here it is, the moment of truth. Can I keep myself together? "Like I said, nothing changed." I feel my heart speed up, hoping he can't see right through me. His lips get tighter.

"Avalon, I know you are lying to me, and I know what is up. Will you please just tell me?"

"If you already know, there's no need for me to tell you."

"So you'll admit something is up."

"No, I never said that."

"If nothing changed, then there's nothing new for me to know or for you to tell me."

"Justin, you're just trying to get into an argument with me at this point."

"No, I'm trying to get you to admit what's going on, but for some reason, you don't want to."

"Justin, I don't know what you're talking about!" I finally yell.

"Avalon, just admit it!"

"Admit what? Justin, nothing has changed! It's just like it always has been!"

"No, it's not; you know that's a lie."

"I don't know what the truth is anymore, so how do I know if it's a lie!"

There's a long pause. In our anger, someone must have bumped the radio because it begins playing Jenna Raine softly in the background, adding a weird feeling to the moment.

"You honestly don't know, do you?" he says, his voice quiet. He speaks as if I might shatter.

"Don't know what?" I ask as my lip starts to slightly tremble. He shifts back in his seat and starts to put the car in gear once again. "Justin, what don't I know?"

"Nothing. If you don't know, I can't tell you."

"Does Ian know?" I immediately regret asking the question.

"I honestly don't know."

"Justin, what do you know that we don't?" I hear the turn signal kick on as he turns back onto the road.

"It's not what I know. It's what everyone knows." I feel the car speed up.

"Everyone, how can everyone know something that we don't?" Once the words leave my lips, I realize what I had said. "Does Austin know?"

"I don't know if he knows. I haven't talked to him in a few days, and honestly, it didn't come up."

"What didn't come up?"

"Avalon," he says, slightly annoyed at my attempt to get information. There's another pause in the conversation, the radio still adding its two cents quietly in the background.

"Hey, Justin."

"Yeah?"

"If Ian did know about the thing we were talking about, would you be able to tell me?"

He let out a sigh. "No, I couldn't."

"That was what I needed to know," I say, feeling my heart ache.

"Are you admitting that you know what I am talking about?"

My mind is spinning. What began as a carefully curated lie might now become a messy, broken, but beautiful truth. "I'm not admitting that I know, but I am admitting that I possibly have an inkling of what you may or may not be referring to."

"Cryptic much," he says with a laugh, trying to lighten the mood.

"You know, the moment I say it out loud, it becomes real." I look down at my shaking hands.

"I know, and I'm sorry for pressuring you."

I nod my head, knowing he means well. "Is it alright if I don't want it to be real yet?"

"Yeah, if you don't want to admit it yet, that's up to you. Just remember." Justin takes a deep breath before continuing his sentence. "You're not the only one who needs to admit it's real."

I nod my head, feeling a little bit of stress relief because if I know one thing for sure, it's that Ian won't admit that any of this is real. If it even is for him.

In the Stars • J. Karter

Chapter 22
Ian

I get home after what feels like a week in the recording studio, but in reality, it was a single day of what could potentially be a two-week process. Typically, I can get it done in five days, but if I stay at this pace, it will take me the whole two weeks.

I collapse onto my couch and turn on the TV. I hear footsteps come to the door and stop at the door frame. "Justin, I don't want to talk about it," I say, rubbing the back of my neck, hoping he won't push the conversation.

"How do you even know what I am going to ask about?"

"You want to ask about what you saw, and I am telling you we're not going to talk about that," I pointedly say, trying to hide the fact that even thinking about it makes my heart skip a beat.

"What if I wanted to talk about your new album?"

"Alright, I'll pretend you are interested in my work. What did you think of the new album? Or at least what you heard of it."

"I'm just curious about what you are going to call it."

"We have a few titles we're working with. Why, do you have an idea? It's out of my typical genre, so we're having trouble naming it."

"Personally, I'm partial to 'An Ode to Audrey,'" he says. I glare at him. He laughs at my disgust with the title. "I'm honestly more interested in where some of the songs came from."

"What do you mean?"

"I mean, I remember you writing 'Roses' for Audrey when we

lived back in Kentucky."

"Okay?"

"It wasn't until I heard 'Eyes,' 'Struck,' and 'Falling' that I realized I didn't recognize any of those songs."

"So, I found them in some old journals," I say, getting off the couch and heading into the kitchen.

"Yeah, something doesn't sound quite right with that," Justin says, following me.

"Why doesn't that sound right?"

"The girl just doesn't sound like Audrey."

"Well, I was sixteen, and my world perspective has changed a bit," I say with a laugh, taking a bite of the sandwich I just pulled out of the fridge.

"Yeah, the biggest issue is that Audrey had blue eyes."

"Okay, good for Audrey." There's a knowing silence between us. "I don't understand what you're trying to get at," I say, trying not to give him the satisfaction of flustering me.

"In the song 'Eyes,' you compare them to wood that was caught on fire by a love that continues to grow warmer." He looks up from a picture of my lyric sheets that he apparently took earlier that day. "So, it was probably about someone else."

I lean up against the counter, becoming more anxious about where he's trying to take this.

"In 'Falling,' you mention falling so hard for someone you can no longer see the pain of the past. All you can see is the bright blue of the future."

"Exactly, bright blue of the future. Audrey."

"Audrey was your first love, dude; you had no pain of the past."

"So I finished that one later; it doesn't matter."

"In 'Struck,' you mentioned something about the pain of seeing someone you can't have."

"Yeah, I saw Audrey every day after she cheated on me with Austin. It hurt a little bit."

"Yeah, but it also mentions that when you were struck, it was like being hit by lightning, nothing like the high school love you had known before."

"I made some revisions; I wrote them when I was sixteen."

"Then explain 'Castle Walls,' where you compare the boy to a knight saving the kingdom from self-destruction."

"I'm not done with that one yet; how did you even find this?"

"So you're currently writing it . . . not about Audrey."

"Okay, maybe that one was written about someone else. It doesn't matter anyway."

"It does when they're written about Avalon."

"Justin, I don't want to talk about it."

"Okay, fine, but remember one thing." I look over at him and watch a mischievous smile creep across his face. "Audrey cheated with Nathan, not Austin."

I look at him, confused, before realizing my slip-up. "Don't you dare tell her," I say in a whisper that almost becomes a growl.

"Don't worry, my lips are sealed," he says with a wink before walking away.

In the Stars • J. Karter

Chapter 23
Avalon

I feel the sunlight start to stream in through my open windows and onto my face. It's been almost two weeks since Ian started recording his new album.

I've been to the studio a few times to watch him record, but mostly, I sit there and crochet while he records. Most days I stay at home and relax by the pool. If you think that you would get bored after four months of literally being paid to do nothing, you would be one hundred percent correct. At this point, I'm considering getting an online degree because I have so much free time.

I roll over and grab my phone off the nightstand. I check the few emails I've gotten and scroll through my social media, which is somehow still gaining popularity even though we haven't gone to any big social events recently. I guess anything seems big to the 457 followers I had when this thing all started, though.

I sit up and put my feet on the cold floor before going to get ready. I fully know I am not leaving the compound today, so I put my hair in a messy bun, grab my old concert t-shirt, and pull on my favorite pair of sweatpants.

I make my way to the music room. I pull out my iPhone and set it up on the music desk (that's the part where you put the music on the piano, something my YouTube studies have taught me). I start the video and match my hands to the hands in the recording, rewinding every once in a while when something doesn't feel right.

I pause the video to rewind it and hear Ian's voice behind me.

"Av, if you wanted to learn to play piano, why didn't you ask me?"

He sits on the piano bench next to me and plays the part I had been struggling to get. I glare up at him. He cracks a smile, "Here, play it with me." He takes my hand and lays it on top of his. He sets his other hand on the keyboard and waits for me to place my hand on top.

I hesitate for a moment. I shouldn't, I know us. I know where this will lead, but I want to. I gently lay my hand on top of his. I see a smile go across his face as he starts playing the piece I've been learning, so I can feel the hand movements. Once the song is over, I remove my hands from the top of his.

"Avalon, why didn't you tell me you were learning piano?" he asks, moving the piece of hair that has fallen in front of my eye.

"Yeah, like I'm going to ask the world-famous musician to teach me piano in his free time."

I see him start to blush a little bit. "Avalon, I would give up all my free time to spend it with you."

I see a flicker behind his eyes, one of the rare moments where I can see his mask crack. He knows what we're doing . . . we both do. I feel my face start to go red. "I'm not going to force you to let me teach you, but if you want, the offer stands," he says, kissing my cheek before getting up and starting to walk out of the room.

"Ian." I spin around, quick to face him. There's a long pause. I know what I want to ask him: 'Why did you kiss me, there are no cameras around?' or 'Why kiss my cheek this time, it's not like you've never kissed me before?' But the only words that leave my mouth are, "Can you show me something else?"

I see a soft smile creep across his lips; it's not like the one he usually gives me. Usually, his smiles feel very warm and inviting. This smile still had warmth to it, but it looked like he was hiding something behind it. "Of course," he replies, walking back over and sitting down next to me.

At this point, I'm not even concerned about what he's trying to teach me. I enjoy watching him play the piano; I enjoy watching his hands move quickly across the keys. But more importantly, I enjoy having him next to me. I don't want him to leave—all I want is for him to sit next to me. All I want is for this moment to freeze in my mind.

I must have lost track of time because the next thing I know, Justin appears in the doorway. "So, did you ask her yet?" he says, a twinkle in his eye. I have a feeling he's been standing there for longer than either of us realized.

Ian scoots a little bit away from me, creating a gap between us, his hands messing up the song he was playing. "No, I completely forgot," he says with wide eyes, turning to face me. "Did you ever decide where you want to go on your trip?"

"Are we seriously back to this? I'm fine here. You don't have to pay for me to go on vacation."

"No, remember, this is a business vacation that we are going on. Did you decide where you want to go?"

"No, we can go wherever. I honestly don't care."

"Perfect, Justin, book the trip," he says with a smile. This smile is back to the one I know, the one that gives me butterflies.

"Yes!" Justin exclaims before leaving the room. The footsteps in the hall make it sound like Justin is running to book the trip.

"So, Justin seems pretty excited about our trip. Where are we going exactly?"

Ian gets up, grabs a chair from nearby, and sets it behind me. I turn around, and he takes my hands. "First, we are flying to New York, and we're going to spend three days there, then we're flying to Kansas City, where we are going to go to a football game, and then we are going to spend three days in Missouri. Each day we are going to go hike a new trail, and then we go back to Kansas City for our next flight to Miami, where we're going to spend a week in a house on the beach before we fly home. Does that sound like a fun trip?"

"It does, but why is Justin so excited about it?"

"The house I like to rent in Miami has five bedrooms. I never liked sharing a room with my brothers, so I always made sure that when we traveled, we always had enough space for our own room. So, as long as it's okay with you— which I really hope it is—Justin is going to join us for that last week in Miami."

"Oh yeah, I'm totally okay with that."

"Perfect," he says, kissing my forehead.

"You must really be having trouble finding my lips today, huh?" The words fall out of my mouth faster than I can process what I'm saying. I feel my eyes widen and my face flush. At this point, I can't tell if it is red or completely white.

He starts to laugh. "Well, let me see if I can find them real quick." His finger finds the bottom of my chin, and he softly guides my lips to his. "Was that better?" he asks.

"Much." I watch him for a moment longer. I see him smile, the smile he gives me when the cameras are off. The one that seems to be reserved for only me and him. I know what we're doing is dangerous, but I don't think I care anymore. *Acting in love is one thing; actually falling for him is something else entirely.*

Chapter 24
Avalon

I don't know if it's just me, but I have never been a fan of airplanes. I enjoy traveling, just not necessarily on airplanes.

"Av, are you ready?" I hear Ian yell from outside my apartment door.

"Almost, just grabbing the last couple of things. How many bags can I bring again?"

"Avy, we're taking the private jet, don't worry about bags," he says, walking into my room. "What bags are ready? I'll take them to the car."

"Those two, I just need to put the last few things in this one." He grabs my bags and takes them to the car. It's not like I can't afford to replace anything that I've forgotten, but it's hard to break old habits from when I couldn't afford to replace what I forgot at home.

I zip up my carry-on bag and grab an over-the-shoulder bag that I use as a purse before walking outside. "I think I have everything."

"Perfect. Now off to the airport," he says, closing the trunk.

"Cass, don't forget your jacket."

"Mom, I can afford another jacket; besides, I already have one packed."

"Did you remember the other thing we discussed, though?" she says, lowering her voice a little bit.

"Yes, I remembered," he says with a smile.

"Okay, good. Have a safe trip, you two," she says before giving us both a hug.

"Are you going to join us down in Florida?" I ask.

"No, not this time, sweetheart. I am going to stay at home and enjoy some time here."

I nod my head. "Okay, I guess I'll see you in two weeks then," I say, giving Grace a hug.

Ian grabs the door for me. I get in the back, and he sits in the front with Justin, who offered to drive us to the airport so we could be a little more under the radar.

We pull up to the jet and walk from the car straight onto the jet. "That's convenient," I say with a smile while Ian and Justin unload our bags.

"Yeah, perks of owning your own jet," he says with a laugh. We take our bags inside, and I stand there for a moment, not sure where I should sit. "Pick anywhere; there are no assigned seats."

I make my way to what would be a normal-facing seat in any other airplane, but instead, I'm facing another seat with a table in between. Ian sits down across from me and pulls out his phone.

"Avy, you okay?" I swallow the saliva that's somehow in my mouth, even though it feels drier than the Sahara.

"Yeah, I'm just not used to flying." I close my eyes and start taking deep breaths as I hear the door to the plane close.

"Avalon, look at me." I feel my legs begin to bounce, and my heart rate begins to speed up. "Look in my eyes," he says as I see a smile creep across his face.

His eyes soften as he looks at me, and the world around him begins to fade into the background. "By the time we are done with this, you will be a pro at flying." I nod at him, feeling my heart rate slow a little bit, but not my legs.

"Now, we just have a six-hour flight. Do you want to look out the window?" I look out the window to see that we are already in the air. "I have some board games or movies if you'd rather do that?"

"What games do you have?"

"Cards, I might have checkers or chess, but no promises that the pieces are all there."

"Let's play cards."

"Perfect," he says, grabbing some cards out of a cabinet and grabbing a soda out of a container. "Do you want anything to drink? Or a snack?"

"Do you have water?"

"Yeah." He grabs a bottle of water and a bag of chips. "Here is your water and your chips."

"Thank you, but I didn't say anything about chips?"

"Yeah, but who doesn't want chips?" he says, putting his package of animal crackers on the table.

"The girl who finds out animal crackers are an option," I say.

He smiles and switches our snacks.

"No, I don't want to steal your snack."

"Honestly, I just wanted to see what you would do. I know how much you love animal crackers."

"How exactly do you know that?" I say playfully.

"You brought animal crackers in your purse to the Grammys."

"Okay, fair point, but they did come in clutch during hour three right after your performance."

"True, I never said they didn't." I start to laugh a little bit. Who would have thought that this crazy situation would start a friendship? After long conversations and a movie, we feel the plane start to land.

"Are you ready to experience New York City for the first time?" I nod my head, getting butterflies in my stomach.

Once we touch down, there is a car waiting for us. We load our bags into the trunk as Ian gets in the driver's seat. We get to a hotel just outside of town. We pull into the parking garage, and Ian's security team hands us the keys to our room.

"One room?" I ask.

"Two-bedroom suite, only one key card, though. I hope that's okay."

"Yeah, that's fine."

We step into the elevator and scan the card that takes us up to one of the top floors. We walk into a hallway that has one door on each side. He scans the card on the left door.

"Welcome to our temporary home," he says as the door swings open. I look and see a full living room and kitchen positioned off to the side. There are two bedrooms, one on each side of the living room, each with a bed. "I'm gonna take the master if that's okay with you?"

"Yeah, of course, you paid for the whole trip."

I grab my bags and start heading for the other bedroom. I open the door and set my bags down just in time to feel arms go around my back. "Hey, Starlight, I've missed you."

No, it can't be. "Austin!" I yell, managing to keep myself in his arms. I turn around and face him; our faces are now only inches apart. "That's still not a nickname," I say quietly. He kisses me in response, but I quickly pull away.

"Was that worth getting on a plane?" Ian asks, appearing in the door frame.

"Yeah," I say with a small laugh, feeling very uncomfortable with the current situation. "I will be with you guys for all three days of the New York trip. I managed to move some things around, and I can be here for most of the day every day."

I force a smile on my face and try to hide the ache that appears in my chest. I should be happy that Austin is here, but instead, all I feel is the sting of what I've lost. I thought this trip was supposed to be our adventure. Just Ian and me.

In the Stars • J. Karter

Chapter 25
Ian

This man is going to drive me insane. I know everyone says your brother becomes your best friend in adulthood, but apparently, those people have never met Austin. I can usually handle his irresponsibility and stupidity, but when it comes to Avalon, I feel like a switch flips in my head.

Last night, I went to bed early because sometimes all I want to do is curl up in bed with a good book and a cup of coffee. When I'm able to binge-read a good book, it usually involves a snack run around the 3 a.m. point. Don't ask me why, it's just what happens.

Anyway, I'm headed for my 3 a.m. snack time when I look at the couch and realize Avalon is asleep on the couch. I walk over and crouch down next to her.

"Avalon, are you okay?" I ask, brushing the hair out of her face.

"Yeah," she says groggily.

"I'm sorry for waking you. I just wanted to make sure you're okay. Why are you out here on the couch?"

"Austin is in my room."

"Why is Austin in your room? He was supposed to rent his own room."

"He's been staying here. I've been taking the couch."

I roll my eyes, frustrated that I've been lied to once again. "Why don't you take my bed?"

"I don't want to sleep with you. I'm sorry."

"I know Avy. I'll sleep on the couch. I'm going to pick you up to take you to bed. Is that okay?"

She nods her head. I put one arm under her legs and one behind her back. She wraps her arms around my neck as she rests her head against my chest. I set her down on the bed and grab my book off the nightstand. "Goodnight, Avalon," I say, shutting off the light.

"Ian, wait." There's an urgency in her voice that cuts through the darkness like a knife. I pause for a moment. "Are you still there?"

"Yeah, I'm still here." I start walking back to the bed and hear her start to move around.

"I think this bed is big enough for both of us."

"I bet it is, Avy. However, I also know that's not really what you want."

"No, I don't want you to lose your bed."

"It's okay. I'll take the couch."

"Are you sure?"

"Yeah, besides, your boyfriend is in the next room over. What would he think of the two of us sharing a bed?" I say with a little laugh, making sure she knows I'm okay, giving up my bed for her. I start heading back to the door.

"Ex-boyfriend." I freeze. My heart starts pounding.

"What?"

"Well, soon-to-be ex-boyfriend."

"Do you want to talk about it?" I ask, walking back towards her.

She sits up and turns on the light next to the bed. "There's no spark anymore."

"Explain?"

"He's moved on. Actually, we both have. We only talk once or twice a month, and that's not any kind of relationship. Even when we talk, it's only for maybe twenty minutes on the phone or an hour over text. We talked about it a little bit this afternoon. We haven't been in a good relationship for a while. It's time to move on, and we both have."

"You both have?"

"Yeah, whether he knows it or not, I know what he's doing on his phone when he thinks I'm not paying attention. That's not the type of guy I want to be with."

"Does he know that you know?"

"About him cheating on me? I have no idea, but I've known for a few weeks now. I've had my suspicions for just over a month, but I've seen at least three different girls he's cheating on me with this weekend."

"Avalon, I'm so sorry."

"It's okay; it makes me feel less guilty for what we've been doing."

That comment cuts deep. *Am I really no better than him?*

"Goodnight, Ian."

"Goodnight, Avalon." She shuts off the light, and I walk out of the room, closing the door behind me. I sit on the couch with my newly acquired snacks and book to distract myself from the emotions that our conversation just stirred up.

After a chapter of trying to get my emotions under control, they finally take over. I walk through the door and turn on the light. "Austin, get up now." I see him set his phone on the nightstand.

"What's the big deal? Can it not wait until morning?"

"No, it can't." He groans and sits up. "I'm going to be real with you right now. It is taking every fiber of my being not to break your nose and send you to the lobby without a key."

"What's the big deal?"

"You've been cheating on Avalon?"

"No, I've been exploring other options while in a committed

relationship. It's called having an open relationship."

"No, it's called cheating."

"Fine, what do you want? I'm tired and want to go to bed."

"You are going to have a conversation with Avalon where you are going to explain that you are the problem in this relationship, not her. I don't want her to think it's her fault that you can't commit to anything."

"So you want me to break up with her?"

"That's one way of looking at it."

"We're already planning on breaking up tomorrow anyway."

"What?"

"We didn't want it to be awkward, so we figured we would keep up the friends thing these past few days, then break up tomorrow morning. Before I drive back to Jersey and you guys catch your flight to wherever."

I shake my head and pinch the bridge of my nose, trying to see the minimal amount of logic in the plan. "Whatever, as long as it's done before we leave New York."

"Why does it matter to you anyway?"

"What?"

"Why does it matter that it's not her fault, and why are you so mad? You were the one who invited me here, remember?"

"I invited you here because I was trying to do something nice for her," I say, feeling myself get more and more agitated.

"Ian, chill, it's not that big of a deal. Avalon and I talked about it. It's mutual."

"That's not the point."

"Then what is the point?" There's a long pause. A look of realization crosses his face. "It matters because you're the other guy." He says it so calm, like he's stating a fact, not unraveling my emotions. "You love her, don't you?"

"That's irrelevant."

"No, that's the only thing that is relevant. You knew I was cheating on her. You made the decision to bring her here; you wanted to see if the two of us were still together." I see a smirk go across Austin's face. "Am I right?" he finishes.

"Austin, me being frustrated with you is about so much more than just Avalon."

"Yeah, I'm sure it is." His voice wavers just the slightest bit. "Did you ever think about the fact that maybe I don't like being the villain in your story?" I watch the performance start to fade for just a moment. "You can be just as misguided as I am sometimes. Don't stand there and look at me like you've never done anything wrong."

There's a long pause. I try to find the words to say, but they never come. I hear his breath catch, and he looks straight at me.

"And don't look at me like I've never given up anything for you." The words flow out of his mouth so naturally, like it's something he has rehearsed a thousand times before. "You guys might just call this act confidence. For me," he swallows, trying to suppress the knot I can hear in his throat, "it's survival."

He looks at me, and just for a moment, I see my reflection. He takes a deep breath, and his mask slides perfectly back into place. "Now, are you going to give me a lecture on how to be a good guy and stay loyal in relationships, or will you be a dear and hit the light on the way out?"

I take a deep breath and walk out the door. I want to linger for a moment longer, hoping I see another glimpse of my brother. Instead, I shut off the light and quietly close the door behind me.

In the Stars • J. Karter

Chapter 26
Avalon

I wake up and look around the room. Memories from the night before start flooding into my head. I sit up almost in shock when I remember the conversation with Ian that lacked a filter that it desperately needed.

Was that real? I think to myself, really hoping that part of that conversation was just a dream. I put my feet on the cold floor and walk into the living room, where I find Ian and Austin sitting at the table with a plate of food set aside for me.

As soon as I enter the room, Austin gets up and gets ready to leave. "Avalon," he says, reaching out to shake my hand. I shake his hand and give him a nod. He pauses at the door for just a second, as though he's trying to commit this moment to memory.

A broken smile appears on his face before he walks out, closing the door behind him. The moment the door closes, I feel a weight lifted. It's the first time I feel like I could be me since we got here.

"All of the work of hiding that relationship for months from the public, and also from Mom and Dad, for it to end with a nod and a handshake," Ian says, looking less than amused.

"What, were you expecting me to be wailing on the ground, pleading with him not to leave me?"

"No, it would have been nice if he had done that, though."

"Yeah, he did that a few days ago, so you already missed it," I say, sitting down as Ian stands up.

"I'm going to pretend that is true just because I like the mental imagery of him in Times Square or in front of the Statue of Liberty on his hands and knees pleading with you not to leave him. Yeah, Statue of Liberty is definitely a better backdrop for that." I roll my eyes as I eat my breakfast. "I still can't believe he was cheating on you."

"I don't know why you are so surprised. Apparently, you were the only one who didn't know. He wasn't the best at hiding it. The first night we got here, we sat on the couch. He had his arm around me, and he scrolled through dating apps as I watched TV."

"I knew; I just didn't want to believe it," Ian says, looking over at me, packing up a few things from the living room.

"I knew it, accepted it, and moved on. It's not hard to leave a relationship when you've already moved on," I say, taking my last bite.

He lets out a sigh. "Just because you can doesn't mean you ever should have had to."

"Says the guy who I've been making out with while the brother I was dating was away for work," I say with a laugh.

"Okay, but that's different."

"Really? How so?" I say, setting my dish in the sink and putting my hands on my hips.

"I pay you for that."

I roll my eyes. "Ian, promise me something?"

"Yeah, anything."

"Never say that again," I say with a slight chuckle.

"Okay, I am aware it came out a whole lot different than it should have, but you understand what I'm saying, right?"

"Ian, I was cheating on him just as much as he was cheating on me. Like it or not, it was mutual."

"I don't think any breakup can be mutual."

"Well, good thing you aren't involved with this one," I say, giving him a quick kiss. I make my way into the bedroom where Austin had been staying. I grab my bag from the corner and move it into the living room area.

"Are you ready for our next destination?" Ian asks, taking my suitcase from my hand and putting one of his bags on top of it so he can pull it out to the car.

"Of course," I say with a smile, trying not to get lost in his eyes. I know my feelings for Ian have been getting stronger, but they seemed to have multiplied from the moment Austin and I decided we were going to call it off. I don't know if it's because I'm finally able to see myself dating Ian or if I'm using it to divert the heartbreak I knew was coming.

We make our way out to the car and load our bags. The jet is already waiting to take us to Kansas City. I'm glad Ian decided to leave in the morning and didn't plan an evening flight out. We load our bags, and I sit back at the same spot I sat in for the flight there.

I know the breakup was mutual, but there's still a part of it that hurts, even if it was my ultimate decision not to let things continue as they were.

"Do you need to talk about it? You still seem really in your head?" Ian asks, looking at me very concerned.

"No, I'm fine. Honestly, just processing." He nods his head. I don't think he believes me, but at this point, I don't know if I believe myself. If this was truly what I wanted, then why does it still ache?

He exhales slowly, like he's been holding something back, and now he's not sure if he should let it out. "Well, I know this probably isn't the best time to do this, but I have something for you." He pulls a box from the bag sitting next to him.

I feel along the black velvet box. I open the lid to reveal a silver necklace with a clef note and a small circle with the letter "I" in it. "Ian, thank you," I say, feeling my heart speed up. A genuine smile finds its way back across my face.

In the Stars • J. Karter

He comes around behind me and helps me put it on. "It's perfect," I say, cradling it in my hands, still looking at the sparkle it gives off. I look up, and instead of getting lost in his eyes, I finally get to see what he looks like when he is lost in mine.

Chapter 27
Avalon

The week in Missouri is exactly what I need. We hike every day, and we stay in a little cabin. Of course, we have to go to some big social events to make sure the cameras see us together, but they are things we get to choose. There are no big mandatory events, just time for Ian and me to spend together and relax.

I think I've been so spoiled that after this next week, I'm not going to want to go back to my little life of isolation in the compound. I know I'm allowed to leave the compound, but I never do. I have no reason to without Ian.

"Are you ready, beautiful?" I see Ian peek his head into the car.

"Ready as I'll ever be," I say with a sigh, disappointed that we have to leave our little secluded paradise.

"Can we make a deal?"

"What is the deal with you saying things like that?"

"I don't know, but I'm happy I corrupted you, and now you say it too," he says with a laugh. "Okay, let me try again." he clears his throat. "I have an idea."

"Okay, I'm listening," I say, leaning over to his side of the car. He gives me a quick kiss before continuing his thought. "If you like it here, why don't we make this a monthly thing?"

"What?" *He wants to come back with me. No cameras, no publicity stunt, just me and him, in our own little world.*

"I can't promise every month, especially with the tour coming up. That reminds me, make sure I tell you about that later. But if you really enjoy it here, let's come back here. At least every few months. Okay?"

I nod my head. "I would really like that." There's a long pause with silence as we stare into one another's eyes. Time seems to stop, and simultaneously, my heart seems to race. I see his breathing get deeper. I notice mine beginning to match his.

Ian blinks, breaking the trance. I see him swallow before smacking his hands on the steering wheel. "Alright, to the airport," he says, still breathing deeply.

He backs out of the parking lot and starts driving down the road. There's a tension in the air that seems to bring a feeling of silence over the sound of the radio. "Avalon."

"Yes?" There's another long pause.

"What are we?"

"Bold question," I say, turning down the radio.

"It's a valid question," he states.

"Why do you ask?"

"I need to know what's real?"

"What do you mean, what's real?"

"What is real, and what is for a paycheck?"

I take a deep breath. "Well . . ." I sit there, watching the fields that we pass by for a moment as I think of an answer that could possibly satisfy him. "I wish I could tell you," I say, my voice quiet and shaky.

"What does that mean?" he asks, a hint of exhaustion creeping into his voice.

"At the beginning, it was for a paycheck. I needed the money and the place to stay, but now I'm not so sure."

"Okay?" he says cautiously.

"Would it be so wrong if I wanted it to be real?" I say, feeling my anxiety level rise.

I begin to think about my bank account as I am speaking. I know I can afford an apartment in the nicer area of town for at least a year or so and still live very comfortably. And maybe with the added fame, I will have enough to book a role because I'm a little more well-known now.

"No," he says.

I feel myself release the air I didn't realize I was holding in my lungs. "Is any of it real for you?" I ask him.

"It is." There's a pause in the car as we drive down the interstate. "Where do we go from here?" he asks me.

"Why are you asking me? Isn't the guy the one who typically makes the first move?"

"This relationship has been anything but typical," he says with a grin.

I begin to turn up the radio once again. "I can agree with that." Instead of music, we hear a voice over the car stereo.

"Justin, how much of that did you hear?" Ian says with wide eyes.

"Enough to know part of my vacation now needs to be spent amending a contract."

"What if there is no contract?" I say.

"What do you mean?"

"We want this to be real, right?"

"Yeah."

"Real relationships don't have contracts."

"She has a valid point," Justin adds.

Ian shakes his head. "I'll call you when we get to Florida."

"Love you too," Justin manages to say before Ian hangs up on him.

"What would this 'real' relationship need to look like?"

"First things first: no air quotes around real. If this is real, it's real. Second thing, I would need a way to make money, but we could come up with something for that."

"Your position would be eliminated, but you could continue to live on the property with us."

"Will your dad let me? If I'm not working for you?"

"It's my house. Who cares what he has to say about it?"

"Okay, so my place to live is now figured out. Money can be figured out later."

My heart begins to race. *Is this it? Is this the moment we decide that it truly becomes real?* "Maybe I could do something on social media for you, and I can get paid that way? Your dad did say he wanted to hire someone on for that."

Ian raises his eyebrow. "I thought the goal was to get you off my payroll."

"The goal is to make this thing real. Which I think it already is. Now we need to get ourselves out of the lovely mess we have so perfectly gotten ourselves into."

We pull up to the airport and bring our stuff onto the plane with us. We sit down, and Ian pulls out his phone, as I feel mine vibrate for the thousandth time since leaving the cabin. Ian glances up at me while he checks or organizes something in a hurry before we take off.

"Who was it?" Ian asks.

"Austin . . . again."

"I should have known," he says, looking annoyed.

I let out a small laugh. "Did you honestly think he would actually leave quietly?" Ian rolls his eyes before responding to something on his phone. "I know one way to get him to leave me alone."

I click on the contact and scroll to the bottom. I tap the *Block* button. "Problem solved," I say with a smile as he slips his phone away and the plane starts moving. I put my hands over his, which are now folded on the table. "So, why don't you tell me about this tour you mentioned?"

In the Stars • J. Karter

Chapter 28
Avalon

Ian talks about his tour for the entire two hours and forty-three minutes of the flight. How he does that without running out of breath, I have no idea, especially when he starts going over his idea for choreography of one of the new songs he just put out. But if there's one thing I've learned about Ian over the past several months, it's that it's next to impossible to get him to stop talking when he's passionate about something.

The moral of that very long story is that it's an eight-month international tour—six months in the U.S. and the other two overseas. We will be traveling for eight months... and I thought two weeks was going to be hard.

I say 'We' because he asked me to travel with him. We're going to look at the dates when things get closer and see if we can make it work with scheduling things, but if I'm helping run his social media, there's a good chance I'll be with him for most, if not all, of the tour. He also understands if I want to take a month off during the tour to be home.

Justin meets us at the airport to take us back to the beach house we rented for the week. Justin helps Ian carry in my bags and sets them down in the foyer. "So what was the contract decision?"

"Don't we need your dad for that?" I ask.

"Nope," Ian says, grabbing a pop from the fridge. "You're paid by my company. Any changes go through me, including termination and title change."

"But isn't it a legal agreement?"

"Leave that to the one with a minor in pre-law," Justin says, setting his backpack on the table.

"You have a minor in pre-law?"

"Yeah, someone had to be the smart one," he smirks. "Bachelor's degree in business management and a minor in pre-law. It was originally meant to manage Austin's career, but instead, Ian now uses it to change contracts behind our dad's back."

Ian raises his glass for a mock toast. "What can I say, I don't like feeling trapped. Who do you think helps me draft all my legal stuff that my dad pretends he understands?" Ian adds.

Justin glares over at him. "Who do you think wrote the contract she originally signed when she took this job?"

"Yeah, that too," Ian says casually.

Justin pulls out his laptop and pulls up the contract that I signed to start this whole crazy thing. "Give me a few hours. If I remember correctly, I left a loophole in here in case this kind of thing happened," he says, studying the contract.

Ian turns and looks at me, then suddenly grabs my hands. "How about you and I go and watch the sunset?"

"That sounds perfect. Let me go change quick, and I'll meet you outside. Sound good?"

He nods as he takes a seat next to Justin. "Second door on the left," Justin yells as I run upstairs. When I get to my room, I find a duffel bag that's sitting on the bed waiting for me. I unzip it and look inside. There are a bunch of clothes and a note on top. I unfold the note and see Grace's handwriting.

Avalon, I bought you some extra clothes for your time in Florida. Have fun, and be safe; I can't wait to see you soon.

Grace

I fold up the letter, set it on the nightstand, and pull out the outfits that Grace bought for me. Over the past few months, I've gotten used to wearing fancier clothes, but I'm still afraid to look at how much some of the clothes that Grace likes to buy me cost.

She always tells me I'm like the daughter she never had, and now she has someone to buy clothes for. All three boys are pretty fashion-forward when they want to be, but most of the time, they stick to fairly casual clothes.

I put on a tank top and a pair of jean shorts I find in the bag, along with a pair of sandals that Grace sent down with Justin as well. I walk out the back sliding glass door and meet Ian outside.

He takes my hand and starts leading me down to the beach. "Sunset walks are one of my favorites. I know it's super cliche, but it's something I've loved since I was a kid."

"We didn't do a lot of sunset walks as kids. I can remember watching the sunset over the fields at Malachi's baseball games, though. If you sat on the top row of some of the bleachers, it looked like you could see for miles."

"Yeah, cause it's Kansas."

"No, well, yes, but not just that. It was only the fields that were just outside of town or in the small towns. The sun would make them almost glow in the summer with the sunset. It's one of my favorite things."

"We'll have to go see it sometime."

"Yeah, we will." There's a short pause. "There was a spot on the farm where you could see the sunset over the wheat fields. When my mom was out of town, my dad would have Auburn and me make a picnic for the four of us, and we would have dinner looking over the fields."

We keep walking down the beach. The sandals are hurting my feet more than I care to admit at this point, but I don't want to ask to stop and take them off.

"Do you want to sit here for a bit?" I nod my head. We sit down on the ground and look out over the ocean, taking in the bright orange sunset. We watch the sunset until it almost entirely fades.

"You ready to head back?"

"Yeah, I think so. I don't want to be out here in the dark."

"Do you want to carry your shoes back, or do you want me to?" I give him a confused look. "You started walking weirdly on the way up here; I assumed it was the new shoes."

"Yeah, it is. I'm not even going to try and lie about this one. Is it safe for me to walk back without shoes?"

"I think so, but at the same time, I could just carry you back if that would be a preferred method of transportation?"

"Ian, it's a fifteen-minute walk."

"And?"

"Are you sure?"

"I wouldn't have offered if I wasn't." He squats down a little bit so I can get onto his back. I carry my shoes as I wrap my arms around his neck and hold on. We make it back to the rental house and find Justin sitting outside, waiting for our return.

"Who's ready to sign some paperwork!" he says, trying to make this process seem a whole lot more exciting than it probably will be.

Chapter 29
Avalon

I sit down at the table across from Justin. "Alright, everyone ready?" he says with a smile. Ian wraps his arm around my waist, a quiet gesture of reassurance. "Okay, so the first contract you signed had you listed as 'personal actress.'"

"That was my official job title?"

"Yeah, and this new one has you listed as a social media specialist. So it's just like any other marketing job."

"Do we have to break the old one?"

"Break? No. End? Yes."

"Huh?"

"Yes, we are going to end your old contract. You don't have to break it. That was the loophole I left in there." He slides a copy of the old contract across the table. He has a few lines highlighted. *In the event that both parties request termination of the agreement, a signed termination form, witnessed by one additional party, shall be sufficient. Termination becomes effective immediately upon signing.*

"That would be why my contract kept getting extended; it never actually had an end date," I say, glancing over at Ian.

"Yeah, someone wanted to make sure that we could keep you on as long as we wanted," Justin says, raising a brow towards Ian. He just shrugs.

"I mean, do you blame me?" Ian says with a laugh as Justin shakes his head.

"So, I need both of you to sign this piece of paper." He slides a termination form across the table.

"Do I need legal counsel for this?" I ask.

"Yeah, I second that," Ian adds. "It's been a while since I signed paperwork and not had a lawyer hovering behind me."

"Are you both over eighteen?"

"Yes."

"Then yeah, you're fine. Feel free to look over it if you'd like."

I look over the piece of paper for a minute before sliding it over to Ian. Ian glances over at me with a twinkle of mischief in his eye. He picks up the paper and tries to hand it back to Justin. "Will you read this before I sign it?"

Justin glares at him. "It's fine, just sign it."

I try my hardest, but a small laugh escapes. Ian hands me a pen, and I sign first. Then I slide the paper over to Ian.

"Legal document," Justin reminds. Ian lets out a sigh, signs it, and hands it back. Justin then slides the new contract over to me. "This one just says that you are working for Ian, doing marketing. It doesn't have a lot of specifics; it just says duties as assigned and that you report to Ian as your boss, not my father." He says all that, looking straight at Ian.

"You can do that?!" Ian says, shocked.

"Yeah."

"And I'm just finding out about this now?"

"Yeah. Because Dad can't stop this one from being signed."

"Fair enough," Ian says with a small shrug. I sign, then Ian signs after.

"Oh, and I gave Avalon the next month off, paid, to learn how to run your social media," Justin says with a sly smile, picking up all the paperwork and grabbing the car keys. "I'm going to go fax these to the lawyer."

Ian and I get up and walk into the living room. "Congratulations to the happy couple," Justin says, opening the door, "and to the lack of a contractual obligation in their relationship." He shoots a smile at the two of us, closing the door behind himself.

I don't leave Ian's side for the rest of the night. Not because I'm scared or nervous of this new step, but because I don't want to be anywhere else. For the first time since I met Ian Karter, I don't have to act. I don't have to pretend to be in love or pretend not to be. For the first time in almost a year, I get to be Avalon Coswell, a girl who has fallen in love with Ian Karter.

Even better than that, I get to be Avalon Coswell, the real girlfriend of Ian Karter.

In the Stars • J. Karter

Chapter 30
Avalon

Ian and I plan to spend the day on the beach today and relax near the ocean waves. Tomorrow, he wants to drive to Orlando and spend the day at one of the theme parks; I don't think he and Justin have decided which one yet. I haven't been to any of them, so I don't care much which one we go to.

I hear a knock. "Are you ready for breakfast, my darling?"

"Yes, as long as I can veto that nickname."

"Understood, your majesty."

"That one is worse," I say with a laugh.

"Okay, back to the drawing board. However, breakfast is ready." I walk downstairs to find Justin finishing up cooking breakfast.

"Good morning, Avalon."

"Good morning. Thank you for breakfast."

"No problem, it's your turn tomorrow though."

"I think I can manage that. Do I need to put in an order for what I'll need?"

"I would. You can check the fridge, but I only bought food for the first day or so."

"Why, you had my credit card?" Ian asks.

"Because I didn't know what y'all wanted for meals, and you can get so picky when you're stressed." Ian shoots Justin a look, and Justin rolls his eyes. "You exhaust me, child."

"I'm older!"

"I said what I said," Justin says before walking out of the room.

Ian and I eat breakfast and figure out the details of our day. We decide to go out for a bit and see the area. Tomorrow, we know we are going to get our pictures taken a lot, but we might as well have some taken of us today. We head to the car.

"Ian, guess what? I just realized something," I say playfully.

"What?"

"We don't have to worry about getting our picture taken together anymore. Right?"

"What do you mean?"

"We can just go out and be a normal couple. No more planning for places with cameras. No perfectly timed arrivals to make sure we are seen together. We can just be us."

"We can, can't we," he says with a smile.

Dating Ian didn't launch me into as much stardom as we originally believed it would, but that's okay with me. I kind of enjoy being able to cheer him on from the background, especially now that I can cheer even louder than before and not have to worry about being caught in any lie.

Truth be told, we do get caught in public, and Ian takes a bunch of pictures with fans. We drive around for a while until our grocery order is filled, and we go pick it up. I know it sounds crazy that I like doing the mundane, but when I haven't been able to for so long, it's nice living with the freedom of not being enveloped in a lie.

We make it back to the rental house, and Ian treats me to a picnic on the beach. If the number of times Justin sneaks behind us is any indication of how many pictures he's taking of our beach outing, we have about a hundred. We finish dinner, and Ian pulls out another velvet black box that I'm seventy-five percent sure Justin dropped off behind him.

"Avalon, I have something that I really need to tell you."

"Ian, I know we don't know when we started dating, but I can assure you this is way too soon for a proposal."

"It's not that, don't worry." He takes a deep breath. "This is a secret I haven't really told anyone, but since we are going to give us a real shot, I want to make sure it is nothing but real."

"Ian, you're scaring me a little bit." He opens the little black box to reveal a bracelet inside. I pull out the small gold bracelet and look at the three letters. C.D.K. "Ian, who is C.D.K?"

"I'm C.D.K." I give him a confused look. "My name isn't Ian Karter. Ian is a nickname that then became a stage name when I started performing. When I became famous, everyone already knew me as Ian, so I let Ian become a persona that I would take every time I took the stage. When I met you, I realized that you didn't make me feel like Ian Karter. You made me feel like Cassian again. My legal name, or my real name, is Cassian Donivan Karter. If we are going to give this a shot for real, I want to make sure you understand that you are dating Cassian Karter, not Ian."

I watch the sun dance off the top of his dark hair. A tension hangs in the air, as if the world around us is holding its breath. "I can't wait," I say, attaching the bracelet around my wrist. I feel him relax as he wraps his arms around me. "Is that why your mom calls you Cass?"

"Yeah, but I have a cousin, Cassidy, so that's how I ended up with the nickname Ian."

I smile at him for a moment. "I love you, Cassian Karter."

"I love you too, Avalon." We watch the sunset for the second night in a row before retiring to our separate rooms. I drift off to sleep, knowing that whatever happens next, I have Cassian Karter with me every step of the way.

In the Stars • J. Karter

Chapter 31
Avalon

I wake up the next morning at 5:23. I like mornings as much as the next girl, but 5 a.m. is a little bit too early for my liking, especially when phone notifications wake me up. I sit up in bed just in time to hear a knock on my door.

"Come in," I say. Cassian and Justin come into my room and turn on my light. "Do you two know why my phone is going off like crazy? It's going off so much, it locked up."

"Did you and Austin pose for any pictures that last night we were in New York?"

"No, we kept a low profile. That was the goal. If we took any pictures, they were on his phone."

"Did he happen to have any pictures of you kissing him on the cheek? Whether from New York or from any time prior?" Justin asks.

"Probably, why? What does this have to do with my phone going crazy at 5 a.m.?"

Cassian sits down on the edge of my bed. He gently rests his hand on top of my blankets. "Someone leaked photos of you and Austin to the press."

"Okay, what's the big deal? We broke up. It's over now," I say, still groggy and not understanding the surprise early morning wake-up call.

"We know that, but the rest of the world didn't know anything was ever happening between you and Austin."

The realization hits me, and I fully wake up. "Everyone thinks I am cheating on you with him, don't they?"

"Yeah, and the press loves a good love triangle, especially when it includes two A-list celebrities and the girl that remains a mystery."

"Okay, so how do we fix this? I'm still a nobody, right? I can disappear for a bit, and maybe this will blow over."

"Avalon, you have over a million Instagram followers."

"No, I had 463 thousand when I went to bed last night."

"And now you have 2.8 million."

"Who leaked the pictures?"

"We're still figuring that out. But I have an idea of who would have posted them," Justin says.

I look towards him. He stands leaning up against the wall, lips tightly pressed together, scanning through things on his phone, trying to figure out what the articles are all saying about the situation. "Found them," Justin says, turning his phone around and showing one of the pictures in question.

"That was from months ago."

"Yeah, but the rest of the world doesn't know that."

I look at the top corner and see Austin's Instagram handle and the three other dots below the picture. "Why would he do this?" I say, putting my head in my hands out of frustration and exhaustion. Cassian starts rubbing my back.

"There's something he stands to gain out of this. I don't know if it's a promotion of his name or an accidental slip of his thumb, but whatever it is, it can't go away now."

"It wasn't a slip of the thumb. The rest of those pictures are recent; that's the only old one."

"I don't know what to tell you, but what I can ask is, do you want a manager?" Justin asks.

"Run that one more time; I'm still trying to wake up."

"Do you want a manager?"

"A manager?"

"Avalon, you went from a nobody to a celebrity overnight. You thought we had people recognizing us yesterday; you haven't seen anything yet. People are gonna want pictures with you and maybe even autographs depending on how invested they feel in the drama."

"The drama that doesn't exist?"

"Exactly."

"I hate Hollywood."

"We all do," Cassian says, patting my back before standing up and walking to the door.

"Is that a yes?"

"Yeah, if I want anyone handling this, I want it to be you." My mind is racing through what of ours Austin could use next. Was this revenge for me blocking him? Was his goal to hurt me by thrusting me into the spotlight?

"Perfect, I'm going to go call Austin and see what pea-sized thought was running through his brain that caused him to post that picture. Also, I'm going to draw up a temporary contract for you and me so I can talk to people on your behalf about this situation." I nod my head as Justin leaves the room.

"Are you okay?"

"I'll be fine." I sit up and run my fingers through my hair. Cassian walks back over to me and wraps me up in his arms. I feel my breathing slow to match his as my eyes close and I sink into him. "Cassian, can you help me with something?" I mumble into his shoulder, never wanting to leave his embrace.

"Yeah?" he says as he pulls away.

"Can you help me understand all the legal stuff that Justin is going to walk me through? I already know I'm going to be lost."

"Of course," he laughs as he starts to leave the room. He pauses in the doorway for a moment. "Oh, and Avalon." I look at the door. "Welcome to the big leagues."

IN THE STARS

www.ingramcontent.com/pod-product-compliance
Lightning Source LLC
Chambersburg PA
CBHW022036220526
45357CB00059B/285